CRUSHED HOPES AND HOPEFUL BEGINNINGS

LIGHT *in the* EMPIRE

CRUSHED HOPES AND HOPEFUL BEGINNINGS

CAROL ASHBY

CERRILLO PRESS

ISBN: 978-1-946139-36-8 (paperback)
        978-1-946139-37-5 (ebook)
        978-1-946139-38-2 (hardcover)

Cerrillo Press
Edgewood, NM

To my children, Paul and Lydia,
for their love, support, and encouragement
and my granddaughter, Payton,
for helping me see
how special the simplest things can be.
And especially to my husband, Jim,
who makes every day better
just by being here.
And most of all, to Jesus.
Soli Deo gloria.

And we know that God causes all things to work together
for good to those who love God, to those who are called
according to His purpose.
Romans 8:28 (NASB)

For there is no distinction between Jew and Greek;
for the same Lord is Lord of all,
bestowing his riches on all who call on him.
For "everyone who calls on the name of the Lord will be saved."
How then will they call on him in whom they have not believed?
And how are they to believe in him of whom they have never
heard?
And how are they to hear without someone preaching?
And how are they to preach unless they are sent?
As it is written,
"How beautiful are the feet of those who preach the good news!"
Romans 10:12-15 (ESV)

Backstory. We all have one, and our future is shaped, at least in part, by our past. But two people can look at the same series of events and see something quite different. Why is that?

What we believe about God and when we started believing it depends a lot on the people we trust at different times in our lives. I was blessed to be raised in a loving home with godly parents. I went off to college believing in God, and what I learned there about the universal chemistry of life and the exquisite complexity of living things, from the level of cells to the total organism, convinced me that I could never doubt the existence of a creator. Jesus promised that the Holy Spirit would come to all who believe He's their Savior, and seeing the Holy Spirit at work in physical miracles and in transforming lives has only strengthened my faith over time.

But many don't grow up in a Christian home. Being told there is no God, that life accidentally happened, that we exist only as long as our bodies are alive, that there's no greater purpose to life than what we make for ourselves—that produces a very different view of the world.

Those of us who believe in Jesus will look for God's hand in the ups and downs of life. We'll remember that He can work all things together for good for those of us who love Him. Those who have never come to know Him see those ups and downs coming from some combination of their own choices and random chance, and no benevolent being is involved.

Learning about a friend's past helps us understand their present. Sharing our own backstory and God's role in it can foster a deeper friendship…or lead to estrangement if our friend is firmly committed to not believing. But even when a friend has no interest in sharing our faith, seeing us live it can lead to questions. It might even offer hope when a despairing friend needs it most.

To fully understand another person is impossible, but knowing the most important parts of their backstory helps, including their relationship with God. That's why many authors, like me, spend time and effort creating a backstory for each main character and for many secondary characters who are important to the story. I need to know my people's past so I can write their future.

Crushed Hopes and Hopeful Beginnings is something new for me: a prequel for my next full-length novel. I hadn't planned to turn a backstory into a prequel, but I felt God's nudges to do it this time. As I was figuring out how Lusario and Caelus came together and developed the friendship that would be so important in the next novel, the ups and downs I dragged Lusario through turned into an adventure worth sharing. His Christian friend, Timon, changed from a single-scene character into a man I would like to count among my own friends.

So, my usual short, narrative backstory grew into this short novel filled with danger for my Stoic hero, unlikely friendships, and courageous faith. All the elements of my full-length novels are here except the love story between a believer and a pagan who decides to believe.

If you're wondering who will be part of that love story, you can find out soon in *River of Life*.

May we all remember when things go wrong that God can bring good out of anything. May we always be a true friend, one who cares enough to share what God can do with those who don't yet know Jesus.

Characters

In Alexandria

Lusario (23): slave from Cyrene who came to Alexandria as Diokles's valet

Diokles (19): Lusario's master in Alexandria, friend of Marcus Florus

Marcus Helvidius Florus (20): Roman who buys Lusario from Diokles

Famulus: Marcus Florus's valet

Achilleus (20): student who is an Alexandrian citizen, a Christian

Timon: Lusario's Greek friend, manservant to Achilleus, a Christian

Zenon: architect who is guiding Caelus's and Lusario's studies

Aemelius Regillus: relative of Paternus who helps Caelus get settled

Gaius Vibius Fundanus: resident of town house where Lusario lived

In Carthago

Caelus Publilius Martinus (18): young Roman who wants to become an architect

Volero Publilius Martinus: Caelus's father, councilman of Carthago

Artoria: Caelus's mother, Volero's wife

Gaius Publilius Martinus: paterfamilias, councilman, and Caelus's grandfather

Juliana: Caelus's step-grandmother, a secret Christian

Martina (17): Caelus's cousin, a secret Christian

Sedulus: steward of Martinus's estate

Gaius Helvidius Florus: councilman of Carthago, Marcus Florus's father

Dromo: steward of the Florus townhouse

Lucius Aemelius Paternus: duumvir of Carthago

In Cyrene:

Philandros: Diokles's father and the original owner of Lusario

Sophos: Lusario's father, a tutor belonging to Philandros

Historical People

Hero (Heron) of Alexandria: renowned mathematician, physicist, and engineer (c. 10 – 70 AD). Most of his writings are his lecture notes from when he taught at the Mouseion in Alexandria in the 1st century AD.

Herodotus of Halicarnassus: historian and geographer (484-425 BC). Called the "father of history." Wrote an account of his travels in Egypt around 454 BC after an Egyptian uprising against their Persian rulers.

Mark the Evangelist: writer of the Gospel of Mark. Egyptian church tradition tells us he was born near Cyrene and returned there after preaching with Paul in Colosse (Colossians 4:10) and in Rome (Philemon 24, 2 Timothy 4:11). He then went to Alexandria, where he founded a church and served as the first bishop there. He was martyred in Alexandria in AD 68.

Plinius (Pliny the Elder): Gaius Plinius Secundus (AD 23/24 – AD 79), author of *Natural History* (*Naturalis Historia*), the encyclopedic work of 37 volumes.

Polybius: Greek historian (c. 200 – c. 118 BC) who toured and wrote about Egypt under the Ptolemies.

Pythagoras of Samos: philosopher (c.570 – c. 490 BC) famous for his contributions to mathematics, astronomy, and the theory of music.

Seneca, Lucius Annaeus (Seneca the Younger): famous Stoic philosopher and playwright (4 BC – AD 65), tutor and advisor of Nero until AD 62, ordered to commit suicide in AD 65.

Strabo: Greek geographer, philosopher, and historian (64 or 63 BC – c. 24 AD). Traveled up the Nile around 25 BC. Wrote about Egypt in AD 17.

Tacitus, Publius Cornelius: highly successful politician (AD 56 – c. 120), regarded as best of the Roman historians, writing between 98 and 113 AD.

Thales of Miletus: philosopher and mathematician (626/623 – c. 548/545 BC).

Vitruvius: military and civil engineer (c. 80–70 BC –15 BC). Served Julius Caesar and Augustus; renowned architect, builder, and general engineer, author of the 10-volume *De Architectura*, a treatise on engineering and architecture.

Zeno of Citium: philosopher (334-262 BC) who founded the Stoic school of philosophy in Athens around 300 BC.

Locations

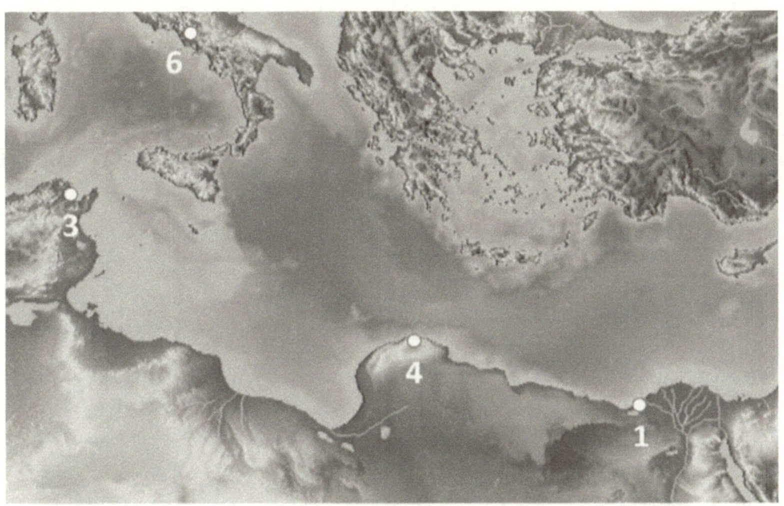

Alexandria (1): built by Alexander the Great as his local capital. Capital of Ptolemaic Egypt and the Roman province of Aegyptus after Octavian (Augustus) defeated Mark Antony and Cleopatra. Port city for 1/3 of the grain supply that fed Rome.

Apollonia: port city serving Cyrene.

Carthago (3): Roman colony rebuilt on the site of Punic Carthage by Augustus. Capital of the Roman province of Africa Proconsularis, which provided almost 2/3 of the grain supply that fed Rome. Near present-day Tunis, Tunisia.

Cyrene (4): Greek city in Roman province of Creta and Cyrenaica, home of the Simon who carried Jesus's cross. Coastal region around Cyrene known as the Pentapolis (Five Cities), near present-day Shahhat, Libya.

Zephyrion: a cape east of Alexandria, site of the Sanctuary of Arsinoe-Aphrodite.

Roma (6): capital of the Roman empire.

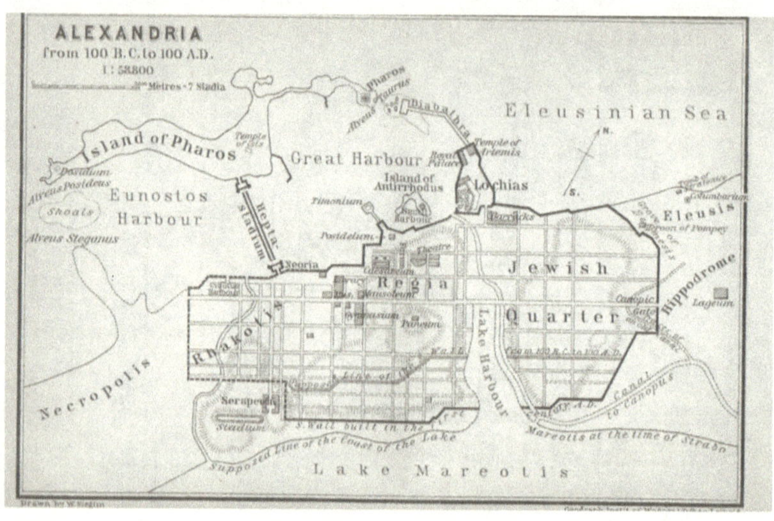

Map of Alexandria from 100 BC to AD 100 by W. Sieglin, 1908
Public Domain

Chapter 1

SERVING TWO MASTERS

Alexandria, Egypt, AD 126

With a satisfied smile that was almost a grin, Lusario set down the stylus and leaned back in the desk chair. A wax tablet lay open on the desk before him, and pride he would never let anyone see grew as he scanned what he'd just written. It was a masterful summary of the argument after the lecture that his young master, Diokles of Cyrene, was supposed to attend that day.

In the hall just west of the Great Library of Alexandria, a less-than-brilliant presentation by a visiting Epicurean philosopher had triggered a sarcastic attack from one of the Stoic philosophers who regularly lectured there. The verbal sparring match that followed had energized the whole room and led to heated discussions outside the hall, where even a slave like himself could take part.

Male laughter drew closer outside the large second-story room that Diokles's father had rented close to the library and lecture halls. Several young men from wealthy families across the Empire shared the elite town house. Too much money, no one in charge whose authority they respected—that was a recipe for trouble, and at nineteen, Diokles didn't even try to resist.

The slightly slurred tenor voice of Diokles was answered by the baritone of his Carthaginian friend, Marcus Helvidius Florus. More nights than not, Florus found some entertainment for them that Diokles's father would not approve.

Each time that happened, Lusario failed in his duty, as defined by his young master's father.

When Diokles turned fourteen, Master Philandros changed Lusario's duties from house slave to his son's personal valet. At eighteen, Lusario found that boring, but it took so little time that he spent most of the day helping his father tutor students for their owner in the school fronting their town house.

An easy set of tasks in Cyrene, but before they sailed for Alexandria two years ago, Philandros had taken Lusario aside to tell him his duties included keeping Diokles from questionable activities with unsavory people in dangerous places. The old master had no idea that his son would form a close friendship with a wealthy Carthaginian who would lead Diokles to all three.

As a mere slave, Lusario could do nothing to stop it. But at least nothing too horrible had happened, and they'd be returning to Cyrene in a few weeks.

With an uneven gait, Diokles entered the room. Florus kept one hand on his friend's upper arm to steady him.

Lusario rose. "Good evening, Master. Shall I prepare your clothes for going out tonight?"

"We're going to a banquet." Diokles waved one hand toward the trunks that held his ankle-length chitons of fine linen and the coordinating embroidered himations that he wore over them. "I want the green set."

After laying the requested attire on the master's bed, Lusario stood with hands clasped at his waist, ready to help Diokles change.

Florus picked up the wax tablet. "What's this?"

Diokles leaned against his friend's shoulder. "Lusario gives me what I need to keep Father thinking I'm as good a student as my brothers were."

The Carthaginian's frown deepened as he read what Lusario had written, and Lusario's heart rate ramped up.

Florus closed the tablet and held it out to Diokles. "Do you understand what he's talking about?"

Diokles opened the tablet and scrunched his face as his eyes tried to focus. "Not really."

"So, what will you do if your father asks you about it when you go home?" Florus crossed his arms.

From everything Lusario had seen, that was never a good sign.

Diokles scratched his head. "I hadn't thought about that."

Florus's finger tapped the tablet frame. "Is everything he writes for you like this?"

"I think so, but I haven't paid much attention." Diokles shrugged.

"Hmph. You'd better start paying attention. You'd be a fool to send something so scholarly to your father. He'd know you didn't write it." Florus handed the tablet back to Diokles.

Diokles whacked the side of Lusario's head with the edge of the wooden frame. "You're supposed to be writing something like what I'd write. Are you trying to get me in trouble?"

Lusario clenched his jaw and squeezed his eyes shut, but only for a moment. He managed to keep from reaching to see if he was bleeding where Diokles hit him. That would invite a second strike.

"No, Master. It was what everyone was talking about after the speakers left the room, so I thought—"

Diokles hit him again with the tablet, and Lusario put his hand on the desk to steady himself.

"That's your problem. You think too much. You're supposed to make it all sound like me, not some real philosopher." He tossed the tablet on the desk. "Do it over, and make it simpler this time."

"Yes, Master."

Florus pushed Lusario aside and seized the tablet. "I can use this version. Father will find the story of two philosophers arguing over such a minor point amusing. I only need to add a little about how I would have liked to see him there to set them straight."

He stroked his jaw. "You are lucky to own a valet who's smart enough to write this. Famulus could never do it. Since this one can, I see an opportunity. Both our fathers expect to hear what we're learning, and we should be going to the same lectures. He could write something like this for me." He waved the tablet at Diokles. "Then make a second version that's fit for your father to read."

Florus poked Lusario's stomach with the tablet. "Can you do that?"

Of course he could. Diokles usually had him do whatever Florus wanted. It was already like serving two masters.

"If you give me the blank tablets, I'd be pleased to do that, Master Florus."

Florus grabbed Lusario's chin and tipped his head back until their eyes met. "And when you go back to Cyrene, you will not tell anyone what you've been doing for us. A valet that can't be trusted with his master's secrets belongs in the galleys or the mines." The Carthaginian's glare reinforced the threat.

"Yes, Master Florus." Lusario cleared his throat. "A valet always protects his master's secrets."

Florus shoved as he released the chin. "Help Diokles change. We're late already."

As Lusario helped his master out of his day clothes and into his evening wear, he glanced at Florus, who still stood by the desk. The Carthaginian was rereading the tablet, nodding as he worked his way down the well-written text. The snap of a tablet closing accompanied Florus's self-satisfied smile.

Lusario drew a deep breath, but stopped before releasing the sigh. It wouldn't be hard to write something to satisfy Florus each day and then simplify it for Diokles. It might even be fun.

It was less than three months until their time in Alexandria ended and they'd be returning to Cyrene. Being Diokles's valet hadn't been unpleasant before they came. Once Florus was no longer around to corrupt the young master, perhaps that would be true again. But valet was only a stepping stone to what he truly wanted.

His father earned a great deal of money for Master Philandros as a highly regarded tutor of elite sons. His own goal these past two years had been to learn what he needed for the same role. He'd done that and more. Once he was home, he'd find a way to convince Master Philandros that he'd have more value as a full-time assistant to his father than as a valet. Maybe someday, the master would let him lead a second school that was his alone.

One corner of his mouth lifted. Maybe even before then, the master would let him and Xenia start a family, like Philandros's father had let Lusario's father do many years ago.

When the two elite sons left the room, he fingered the lump where the tablet hit. It hurt to touch, but his fingers came away without blood on them.

A man could put up with a lot if it helped him reach his goal. He'd decided long ago to let the charioteers at the circus be his model. It wasn't your position at the end of each lap that determined your future. Only where you were as you crossed the finish line mattered.

Chapter 2

All He Had Left

Two weeks later

Lusario set the scissors by the wash basin on the small table. It took more skill than he had to make Diokles's thin beard look as manly as his young master wanted. Most young men looked better clean shaven like Trajan, not bearded like Hadrian. Even when a beard grew fast and thick like his did, clean-shaven took less time.

But this morning, Diokles hadn't uttered any of his usual complaints.

Something was wrong.

Last night, his master had left with Florus, but for the first time, they hadn't returned together. As the last stars disappeared and the sky turned lighter gray, Lusario had dozed off in the wicker chair, waiting to help Diokles prepare for bed. He awoke when his master kicked his shin and slapped his ear to get him out of the chair.

Diokles had returned sober. That was another first since he started spending evenings with Florus.

Lusario expected his master to collapse on the bed and sleep until almost dinner time. Instead, he sank into the wicker chair and demanded the usual morning grooming.

Each set of footsteps approaching on the balcony caused Diokles's head to jerk toward the door. Lusario had almost snipped a section of beard too close with his last jerk. As he drew the freshly sharpened razor up Diokles throat to cut away the sparse hairs, his jaw clenched. Tending a jumpy, angry master could be dangerous. The slightest nick, and Diokles might call it attempted murder.

He finished the last stroke and released the breath he'd been holding. As he swished the hairs off in the bowl of water, Florus ambled through the door.

"You should have come with me. The dancing girls were worth what they cost, in more ways than one."

With steepled fingers, Diokles rubbed the sides of his nose. "I was a fool not to." Eyes closed, he tipped his head back. When he turned his gaze back on Florus, a deep sigh drained Diokles's lungs. "I should have quit when I was only a little behind, but I thought my luck would change. It did for a while, and then…"

"How much did you lose?" The smile Florus wore when he entered flipped to a frown.

"Enough that I won't even have the money for passage home after I settle my other debts here. Speratus said he wanted the money right away since he knew I was about to go home."

He leaned forward, elbows on his knees, and buried his face in his hands. "What am I going to do?"

Florus rested his hand on Diokles's shoulder. "How much do you owe, and how much do you have?"

"About 1800 drachmas. After I pay for passage home, I'll only have a little over two thirds of that."

Florus blew out a breath. "So, you need about six hundred more." He wiped his mouth with the back of his hand. "Father makes me send him careful accounts of what I spend here, and I have about a thousand left of what I brought with me. That's more than I need to buy passage and cover expenses until I sail home a few days after you leave. If it were up to me, I'd just give you the money, but everything I treat as mine is really his. He'd be furious if I did that."

"I know you'd help if you could. If I was staying here longer, I'd ask Father for help. He'd be angry, and who knows what he'd do when I get back home. But I think he'd send someone with enough to clear my debts and get me home. He'd be too embarrassed not to. He'd hate to have anyone in Cyrene learn about my money problems."

Florus pinched his lower lip. Then his calculating eyes turned on Lusario, and the worry on his face turned into smug satisfaction.

Lusario's stomach clenched, and he started to breathe like he'd just run a mile. He focused on slowing it down before either noticed.

"Father owns everything I treat as mine, and no Roman son can sell anything important without his *paterfamilias's* approval." Florus rubbed his jaw as he continued to contemplate Lusario. "But you're not Roman. So, can you sell anything you have here?"

"I suppose, but I don't have anything that valuable."

"But you do." Palm up, Florus extended his hand toward Lusario. "You have a valet that I'd be willing to pay 600 drachmas for. So, I wouldn't be giving you Father's money. I'd be adding a slave to his household. He can recover the money by selling him again after I go home."

Diokles perked up, and Lusario's stomach curdled. It was all he could do not to vomit.

He clenched his jaw and swallowed the desperate "no" he almost shouted. If Diokles said yes, all his plans, all his dreams of a future working with Father and raising a family with Xenia were destroyed. He'd never even see them or his sisters again. He'd end up in Carthago, never to return to Cyrene.

And belonging to Florus—he'd seen how he treated Famulus. Any spark of hope for a better life that his valet might have cherished had long since been quenched.

He fought to keep the fear and despair off his face. Both men expected their slaves to act like well-trained dogs, coming at the snap of their fingers and eager to obey.

"You'd buy him?"

As hope replaced desperation on Diokles's face, black despair filled Lusario's heart.

"Certainly. You're my best friend, and friends should look out for each other, even if they aren't going to be together all the time. He can even keep serving you until you sail."

"Then he's yours." A grin split Diokles's face before he turned his gaze on Lusario. "Find out how to draw up the sale papers and have them ready for me by this evening."

Lusario swallowed the lump rising in his throat, then tipped his head. "Yes, Master."

Florus slapped Diokles's shoulder. "Let's go get breakfast. Then I have some ideas for how to spend today that I think you'll enjoy."

As they headed out the door, Florus glanced back over his shoulder. "You can keep your name when you make the bill of sale."

Lusario sank into the wicker chair as their happy voices faded away. Keep his name. It was all he had left of everything that he'd been and all that he'd hoped to become.

He buried his face in his hands, and his shoulders shook with silent sobs.

Chapter 3

Someone to Help

Lusario trudged back from the agora, where he'd found a scribe who knew how to write up a bill of sale for a slave. It lay atop the blank papyrus sheets in his satchel. How fitting. That single sheet erased everything that mattered in his life, making it as blank as the sheets that he'd never write on.

It wasn't fair. He'd always served faithfully, never slacking off, doing everything to the best of his ability. Master Philandros had appreciated that. He'd even trusted Lusario with watching over his son for the last two years. When the time came, he would have made Lusario a tutor, given him Xenia as his wife, helped him become as sought-after as Father was for teaching the elite of the city.

One night of drunken gambling by Philandros's worthless son, and everything he'd counted on was stripped from him. All that he'd learned to prepare for that life…what did it matter now? He'd never get to use it.

But as he walked past the main building housing the lecture halls, he slowed. Then he squared his shoulders and raised his chin. He still had a few more days before he was dragged off to Carthago and sold to do who knew what. Since his father began teaching him as a boy of seven, learning for its own sake had been his greatest source of pleasure. Until Florus ordered him to stop, he'd keep coming to the lectures because *he* wanted to, not because the irresponsible youth he served needed something to tell his father.

He turned in to take his usual seat at the rear. For a few more days, he could be a scholar, not just some man's slave.

The seats at the front where the highly respected scholars sat were already occupied, and the next rows where the wealthy students listened were filling fast.

Timon settled into the seat next to Lusario while his master worked his way forward to sit where Florus and Diokles should have been sitting if they ever came.

"Do you suppose we'll see as good an argument today?" Timon nudged Lusario's shoulder.

Lusario tightened his lips and shook his head. The last thing he wanted was for the always-cheerful Timon to try to drag him into a conversation he would have enjoyed yesterday. The bill of sale in his satchel had sucked any enjoyment out of life.

He jumped when Timon placed his palm on Lusario's upper arm. "What's wrong?"

His mouth opened, but no words came. How does a man tell someone that all he'd wanted for his life had been rendered impossible by a drunken youth and his rich companion who thought what he'd done was a noble act to help a friend?

The lecturer for the day had just stepped into place, and Lusario tipped his head toward the platform, "If you really want to know, ask me after he's through."

He'd whispered because the master of the hall was introducing the speaker. Silence was expected from the slaves and servants who sat along the back wall.

Timon whispered back. "I will."

Try as he might, Lusario couldn't keep his mind focused on the lecture. He'd felt like nothing could be done because no one in Alexandria cared enough to help him. But sitting next to him might be the first step to solving his problem.

How much was safe to tell Timon? There was nothing a manservant could do himself to help. But would he maybe know someone in Alexandria who would be willing to buy a highly educated valet who could also work as a tutor? Would Timon's own master even buy him? Timon was well fed, wore clothes better than many free men had, and never had bruises or cuts, so his friend's master must be a good one.

The questions and counterarguments began. Even though this was normally Lusario's favorite part, it was taking too long. His knee started bouncing, and he willed it to stop.

At last, the speaker stepped down from the platform, and Timon's master, Achilleus, joined the other students waiting to speak with him.

Timon tapped Lusario's shoulder. "Come outside and tell me."

They wove through the crowd until they reached a bench against the outside wall. Timon sat and patted the spot next to him. "What's happened?"

Lusario drew a deep breath and, with eyes closed, blew it out slowly. When he turned his gaze back on his friend, Timon's usual smile had vanished.

"You know how I've been coming to all the lectures so I could be a tutor like my father someday." His jaw clenched. "Diokles lost more than he had gambling, and he had to pay it before we leave for Cyrene. So"—he ran his fingers through his black curls—"he sold me to Florus to get the 600 drachmas he didn't have. I'll be going to Carthago with that son of a…Roman instead of home."

He closed his eyes and shook his head. "Everything I ever hoped for, all that I planned, everyone I love back home—I've lost it all."

Timon's hand rested on his upper arm, and Lusario opened his eyes. "I know it looks hopeless, but maybe Master Achilleus will have an idea about what to do."

"I don't think anything can be done. I belong to Florus's father now, and he's in Carthago." His hand rested on the satchel. "The bill of sale is in here."

"We'll ask my master anyway." One corner of Timon's mouth lifted. "He has a knack for finding a solution when other men can't."

When Timon's master stepped through the doorway, Timon stood and raised one arm. Achilleus raised a hand in response and walked over. When he was ten feet away, Lusario rose as well.

Achilleus's gaze moved from Timon to Lusario and back. "Why the solemn faces?"

Timon rested his hand on Lusario's shoulder. "Lusario was about to go home to Cyrene to become an assistant tutor with his father. That was going to let him marry a young woman of the household and maybe earn enough someday to buy his freedom. But his master lost too much gambling, and Florus gave him money in exchange for Lusario to pay his debt. Now my friend will have to go to Carthago with Florus instead of home to Cyrene." Timon massaged his neck. "Unless you can do something."

After handing Timon his wax tablet, Achilleus pinched his lower lip. "So, you want to go with Diokles when he returns to Cyrene."

"More than anything else in the world. Everyone I care about is there, and I'm sure Master Philandros will make me a tutor so I can buy my freedom someday."

Achilleus stroked his bearded jaw. "Will Diokles be at the baths after lunch?"

"He and Florus almost always go there after they eat." Lusario's heart rate rose. Was Timon's master actually going to help?

"How much did Florus pay for you?"

"Six hundred drachmas."

Through pursed lips, Achilleus blew out a slow breath. "I can't promise anything, but I'll see what I can do."

Achilleus tipped his head toward the street. "I'm expected elsewhere now. But I'll look for your master when I go to the baths this afternoon." He turned and strode away.

Timon slapped Lusario's shoulder. "If anyone can help, it's him." Then he trotted after Achilleus.

With the back of his hand, Lusario rubbed his mouth. What was Timon's master planning to do? What were the chances it would work?

Baths of Alexandria

Florus walked across the mosaics of frolicking dolphins and down the steps into the *caldarium* pool. When he sat on the side-wall bench, his muscles relaxed as the hot water swirled across his shoulders. When Diokles settled in beside him, a sigh escaped. For more than a year, their friendship had grown and deepened. When each returned to their home city in a few days, would they ever get to lounge together like this again?

Diokles rested his head against the edge of the pool to stare at the arched ceiling. "When we both go home, I'm going to miss this."

"I'll be leaving only a couple of days after you. Maybe you can visit Carthago soon. It's only a week and a half by sea, and you can stay as long as you want."

"I'd like to. My brothers travel some, but it's usually because Father entrusts them with family business." Diokles ran his fingers through his sweat-dampened hair. "I hope he doesn't ask me about all the things I'm supposed to have learned here. Having Lusario write those letters for me seemed like a good idea when I started. But if Father figures out it wasn't me writing them…"

"You can make something up if he does ask. Your valet is going home with me, so he can't betray you. There should be no problem."

"Probably not, as long as my brothers aren't there to contradict me. Father's not a scholar himself."

Florus's smile turned into a frown when Achilleus stepped into the pool next to Diokles and sat on the edge. Ever since the Alexandrian told him to keep his hands off the pretty Egyptian who served the wine at his favorite taberna near the hippodrome, he couldn't stand the man. Florus was a Roman, and an Egyptian servant, whether slave or free, had no more right to tell him not to touch her than one of his father's slaves.

Achilleus had gripped Florus's wrist and pulled his hand away before stepping between them. He'd had the gall to tell him she was only there to serve the drinks and to leave her alone. No Alexandrian had a right to tell an elite Roman what to do, no matter how important his family might be in the city.

"I was hoping I'd find you here, Diokles." Achilleus shifted to face Florus's friend. "I hear you're returning to Cyrene."

"I am. This week, in fact. I've finished my studies, and it's time to go home."

"Going home—that's what I hoped to discuss with you. Your valet and my manservant met while waiting for us at the back of the lecture halls. They've been good friends for some time, and they just told me you weren't taking Lusario home with you."

Diokles tensed, and Florus twisted on the bench to face the Alexandrian. What his friend planned to do was none of Achilleus's business.

"I'm not." Diokles shrugged. "What about it?"

"He wasn't sure how to tell you, but Lusario really wants to go back to Cyrene with you. Your father's household is all he's ever known, and his loyalty to your father and your whole family is obvious. He'd hoped to serve there his entire life." Achilleus smiled, but it looked more patronizing than friendly.

"Parting with a slave as smart and loyal as he is—it's not something most owners want to do. I know his sale price paid your gambling debt, but wouldn't your father send the six hundred drachmas to Florus's father if you asked after you get home? Then Lusario could go home with you and continue serving his household."

Diokles squeezed the back of his neck. "I suppose Father might be willing to do that. Lusario had more than valet duties before I came here. He helped his father earn us money as a tutor."

Florus clenched his jaw. He'd solved his friend's problem by buying his slave. What business was it of this arrogant Alexandrian after he'd already taken care of what Diokles needed? How did he know it was six hundred drachmas, anyway?

"Diokles's father might be willing, but what if mine isn't?" Florus tipped his head to look down his nose at Achilleus. "Father would be furious if I show up in Carthago without the slave and with only the hope that someone might refund what I paid for him. Even an Alexandrian like you should know enough about Roman law to know the *paterfamilias* owns everything his son uses like it was his own. Father's name is on the bill of sale."

Achilleus drew back. "I see your point." He stroked his thick, precisely trimmed beard. "But there's an easy solution. I will give you the price you paid for Lusario so you'll have all the money you should be taking back to your father." He turned a smile on Diokles. "I would only need a promise in writing from Diokles that his father will repay me. We're all men of honor, so I trust that he'll fulfill his son's commitment."

Why was Achilleus proposing this? Was he trying to make Florus's own generosity to a friend seem like nothing at all?

"The slave belongs to my father now, not me, not Diokles. Without Father's express permission, he's not for sale. That should be simple enough for even you to understand."

He flared his nostrils as if some odor offended him. Achilleus should have felt the full insult. So, why did he still sit there, smiling as if he hadn't seen?

"So, what's done is done." Florus narrowed his eyes. "But even if he were for sale, I wouldn't sell him to you."

Diokles's eyes widened as he turned his gaze from the Alexandrian to Florus. Then they narrowed.

Florus clenched his teeth. How could his best friend be looking at him like that? He'd given him a large sum of money to pay off his debt. Did Diokles even appreciate what he'd done?

How dare that slave tell anyone that he didn't want Florus to own him? It was even worse that it was Achilleus, who'd already had the gall to tell him to keep his hands off a mere Egyptian who didn't welcome his attention. Now he was trying to tell Florus what he should do with his own property.

Achilleus stood and stepped out of the pool. "In case you change your minds, the offer stands until Diokles sails. I'll be here every afternoon if you want to find me."

"We probably will, too." Diokles offered him a much-too-friendly smile.

Before Achilleus turned toward the exit, his smile was at least as warm. "I wish you both a safe trip home."

As the Alexandrian strode away, Florus stood. "Ready for a swim? Or a race? Maybe you'll beat me this time."

Diokles's chuckle declared all was still well between them. "Maybe, but we both know that's not likely."

With a friendly slap to the arm, Florus led them toward the large pool outside.

Diokles had been too kind a master. He'd let Lusario be too independent. A master should never let a mere slave presume that what he wanted might matter. But the too-clever Cyrenian valet would soon learn what it meant to be a Roman slave, and Florus would enjoy teaching him.

Chapter 4

Why Would He Help?

Diokles's lodgings, late afternoon

When Lusario climbed the stairs to their balcony room, he was well ahead of the time Diokles expected him to be there to help prepare for the evening's entertainment. Would Timon's master have found time to explain how much he wanted to go home to Cyrene? Would Diokles have cared enough to do something about it?

When he opened the door, his master was already there. He sat on the desk chair, facing Florus, who had his back to Lusario.

Maybe it was a good sign that Florus was there. He would have to agree to Diokles taking him home.

When Florus turned, a shaft of fear pierced Lusario. He'd seen Florus angry before, but his eyes had never blazed with pure fury.

Two hands gripped his throat before Florus slammed him against the wall. As the Roman squeezed, Lusario fought the urge to defend himself. Striking a master, even in self-defense, could put him in the arena to feed the beasts.

Diokles leaped up and grabbed Florus's wrist. "Let him go. He doesn't deserve this."

The pressure on his throat relaxed enough for him to breathe, but Florus's thumbs still pushed into his throat enough to hurt.

Diokles tugged, but not enough to break Florus's grip. "He was born in my father's household, and he's always done everything we asked of him well. He's always been allowed to do other things when he finished his assigned work."

He tugged again, to no avail. "He usually sat at the back with Achilleus's manservant. They probably talked, and the manservant probably asked Achilleus to help him go back with me. If you didn't tell him you wouldn't sell him, you can't expect him to know he shouldn't tell someone he might be for sale. He knew you didn't really want him. You just bought him to help me."

With hands still around Lusario's throat, Florus slammed his head against the wall.

Lusario had read that a man saw stars when struck hard enough. He knew the truth of it now.

Then Florus released him. His index finger rested against Lusario's forehead, and he pushed him into the wall again. "Don't forget who owns you now." He turned to Diokles. "I'll let him forgetting his place pass…this time. As you say, I haven't told him what I expect yet. I said he could keep serving you, so he can do what you let him until you leave."

Florus marched out of the room, and Lusario felt his throat. What would Florus do after his final wave to his friend on the quay and Diokles would no longer be there to stop him?

"We're going to a farewell banquet tonight. Have my evening clothes ready when I return. Blue this time." Diokles sauntered after Florus, but he paused in the doorway.

"Tomorrow morning, find a ship going to Cyrene this week and book me a cabin room on it."

"Yes, Master." Lusario touched the back of his head. A bump was already forming.

Within days of Diokles sailing home, Florus would be going back to Carthago. Less than three weeks on the ship, and Lusario would be in a strange city without a single friend and no idea of what awaited him.

He opened the trunk and pulled out the light blue chiton and darker blue himation. With shoulders sagging, he inspected them before he laid them on Diokles's bed. The linen was wrinkled from being at the bottom of the trunk, but Diokles wouldn't mind. His new Roman master would strike Famulus for offering him a tunic that wrinkled, even though there was no place in their lodgings to take out wrinkles and his toga would cover all but one shoulder, anyway.

Famulus was as good a valet as Lusario had seen. Florus wouldn't need another. So, what would Florus want him to do?

Three and a half weeks, and most of that on a ship where Florus could watch him constantly. Maybe he could make it that long without getting Florus too angry. But if past experience predicted the future, he wouldn't bet on it. Famulus had a fresh bruise or black eye at least once a week.

He stood by the window and let his gaze drift across the city he knew so well. Would he even end up in Carthago, or would he be sent to a country estate? He only knew urban life. He wasn't fit enough to be a farm slave.

What kind of man was his new owner? Hot-tempered with a

cruel streak like his son? Or was he as different from Florus as Master Philandros was from Diokles?

Maybe he'd be a man who didn't like to waste what he owned, and he'd put his newest slave to work doing something that used his talents. Or maybe he left control of the slaves to his steward, and the steward knew value when he saw it.

What the future held…it looked bleak right now, but even the longest night was followed by the pale light of dawn.

He closed his eyes and shuddered.

Or it ended in death.

The lecture halls of Alexandria, the next morning

As Lusario approached the main lecture hall, the anticipation that had quickened his stride each morning was gone. A few more days, and he'd never again enter the room, take out papyrus and pen, and greet Timon before hearing one more talk that expanded his mind. That all would have ended if he'd been going home, but what would have been bittersweet was only bitter now.

When Lusario had gone to the harbor that morning, his old and new masters still lounged in the triclinium, enjoying a leisurely breakfast with the other elite students who lived there. What they planned for the rest of the day…he didn't know and didn't care.

Many ships traveled between Alexandria and Cyrene, so finding a cabin room for Diokles had been easy. It was tempting to delay his departure until the end of the week, for that would mark the end of Lusario's own time with the friends he'd made in a city he loved. But when Florus came to the door to get Diokles for breakfast, he'd ordered Lusario to arrange his passage as well and be quick about it.

Passage for three with Florus and Famulus in a cabin room with bunk beds left him sleeping on deck. But since he would be arranging the baggage pickup as well, he could add his one small chest of personal items, including the many sheets of papyrus notes and a handful of wax tablets that he valued most. He could get them to Carthago, but would he be allowed to keep them once he was there?

As he'd paid for the second ship, despair had wrapped around him. But like a gladiator who entered the arena knowing death might await him, Lusario struggled against it. Once a man gave up hope, he might as well curl up and die.

He entered the hall and settled in next to Timon.

"I wasn't sure you'd make it today." Timon greeted him with his usual smile.

"I had to arrange passage on two ships." With the tips of his fingers, he touched his bruised neck. "I'll be on the one going to Carthago."

"That could still change." Timon shifted in the chair to face him. "Diokles wanted to take you home with him. Master Achilleus offered to pay Florus what he'd given for you so his father would get his money back instead of a new slave when Florus went home. Your master in Cyrene only has to pay him back after Diokles gets there. He was surprised that Florus wouldn't take the offer right away. There was no good reason for keeping you. But maybe he'll change his mind. Master told them the offer was good until Diokles actually leaves."

"That won't happen now. Florus does whatever he wants, and he expects others to yield to his wishes. He picked my master as his closest friend because he could control him like a puppet. He was angry that I'd told anyone I didn't want to go with him. I found out yesterday why his valet is so careful around him." He felt the bump on the back of his head, then the bruise on his throat. "Famulus might be thinking Florus has someone else to take his anger out on now. But he probably has enough for both of us."

Timon's eyes widened before he lowered his gaze to their feet. "I'm sorry you have to put up with that. I wish you served someone like Achilleus instead."

"So do I, but Florus had better never find out I said so."

Lusario looked away so Timon wouldn't see how much he envied him.

The Romans would say Fortuna had smiled on Timon when he got Achilleus as master. The Greeks would claim it was Tyche who granted him favor. His Egyptian friends would credit Shai, the god of fate who determined the span of a man's life.

One corner of Lusario's mouth lifted. The great writers of history claimed the favor of the gods decided the fate of kings and nations, but did any god ever smile on a slave?

"Please tell your master how much I appreciate that he tried to help. For him to offer to pay Florus what I cost him, even as a loan until Master Philandros could repay him…" Lusario's gaze settled on Achilleus where he stood talking with friends. "I'm nothing to him. We'd never even spoken before yesterday. So, why would he do that?"

Timon's mouth opened, as if he intended to speak, then closed. His eyes narrowed as he rubbed under his chin. Then he shut his eyes, and as he drew a deep breath, his smile grew.

"We've come to know each other well these past two years, and I know you're a man I can trust. I almost told you something several times, but someone always interrupted before I could start. So, I knew it wasn't time, but now it is. But if I tell you, you can't tell anyone else, especially not Florus. He'd want to use it to strike at my master. Diokles can't know because he'd tell Florus."

"I'll never tell either of them. You have my word."

A single nod signaled Timon's acceptance of the promise. "Master Achilleus tried to help because we're told we're supposed to love other people as much as we love ourselves. He wanted to spare you from losing your home and family and all you'd dreamed of."

Lusario drew his head back. "Told by whom?"

"Our God." Timon's voice was a near whisper. "We follow Jesus of Nazareth, and he said we are to obey the two greatest commands. The first is to love God with all our heart and mind and soul and strength. The second is to love other people like we love ourselves. The kind of love Jesus was talking about is *agape*…unconditional love."

"Agape? I know about three different kinds of love. *Phileo, storge*, and *eros*—I've felt all of those. I never heard of agape." Lusario had lowered his voice to match Timon's.

Timon glanced around to see if anyone was listening. On either side and below them, no one sat near enough to hear. "Love for your friends, love for your family, the love for a woman that starts with desire—those are only feelings we have toward other people. The agape kind of love God calls us to isn't a feeling. It's a decision we make followed by what we do. It's wanting what's best for another person, even when that costs us something. It's doing what we can to help when it's needed, even if we'd rather not. It doesn't depend on what they do or how we feel about them."

Timon turned his face away and stared at something across the room. As soon as his gaze returned to Lusario, he lowered his chin and rubbed his palm with his thumb.

"These past two years…we've shared phileo. I'm going to miss seeing you here, listening to the best lectures together, talking about what we've learned. I've never had a friend like you before." Timon's usual smile faded. "If you can, let me know where to write to you. Master would give me the money for sending you letters. But I'll understand if you can't."

"I'd like that." Lusario forced a smile. That Florus would allow it was beyond what he could believe.

"Master Achilleus…his decision to help you was agape. He'd do it even if Diokles's father wasn't likely to repay him."

The master of the hall stepped onto the platform. When he raised his hand for silence, Lusario wasn't sorry. Timon's words of friendship had pricked his heart and added one more loss to the too-long list he tried not to think about.

Three more days, and Diokles would be boarding a ship for Cyrene. Five more days, and he'd be on a ship to Carthago.

Alexandria had been all he'd hoped for and more. Whatever came next, he'd hang on to these memories as if they were the richest treasures.

His jaw clenched. Memories were the only treasures a man could count on when another man owned his body. But no matter what Florus or his father did with him, he'd remember Timon and this time when he felt almost free.

Chapter 5

Reaching Carthago

Harbor in Alexandria, three days later

Lusario stood on the quay, arms crossed, as he watched two dock slaves carry the largest trunk up the gangplank and down into the hold. Giving Diokles the receipt he'd need to claim it at the end of the voyage would be his final act of service as a Cyrenian slave. Henceforth, he was only a piece of Roman property. What that would mean…he shuddered.

"I hoped you'd be here." Timon's voice triggered a smile as Lusario turned.

"Aren't you supposed to be at the lecture hall?"

"Master Achilleus was summoned by his grandfather, and we're going upriver to the family estate first thing tomorrow. I wanted to see you before you left, so he told me I should come today."

"I'm glad he did." Lusario fixed his eyes on the receipt as he folded it. Farewells hurt, but not getting to say them hurt even more.

"He said I should tell you we'll keep praying for you to end up with something better than you're expecting. Last night, I sensed our prayers will be answered. I think you'll get as good a master as I have with Achilleus. After that…" He shrugged, and the smile that

31

greeted Lusario each time they met appeared. "Only God knows the best way to answer our prayers. I'll be praying for God's best for you to come quickly. I don't know what that could be, but I'm certain it will come."

He pulled Lusario into a quick embrace, then slapped him on the arm. "I hope to hear how our prayers have been answered soon."

Lusario clenched his jaw. Tearful farewells were for women, and he didn't want that to be his friend's final memory of him. "I'll try to write, if it's allowed and I can find the money to do it." He tipped his head toward the ship. "I have to help Diokles get settled. Farewell, my friend."

He spun and headed up the gangplank. From the top, he glanced back.

Timon still stood on the quay. He raised one hand, then turned and slowly walked away.

Lusario squared his shoulders and went into the cabin to help his old master's son one last time.

He handed the receipt to Diokles. "You'll need this in Apollonia to reclaim your trunk. There should be a carriage service near the quay to take you from there to Cyrene."

Diokles took the receipt and scanned it. He avoided looking Lusario in the eyes.

"Master Florus said he'd be here shortly to keep you company until you sail." Lusario cleared his throat. How do you say goodbye to the one who'd taken you into a world filled with wise men's thoughts and dreams of a future before that person's careless stupidity destroyed your life?

"I'm Master Florus's now, and he told me to help Famulus with final arrangements. So, this is goodbye. I'm glad I got to serve you in

Alexandria. Going to the lectures and writing things up for you… it's been my greatest pleasure. Please tell my father and sisters I'll always be thinking about them. If it's possible, I'll write to Father sometime."

Diokles turned regretful eyes on him. "I tried to persuade Marcus to take the money from Achilleus, but you know how he is once he sets his mind on something."

Lusario only nodded. Anything he said might only make matters worse if Diokles repeated it to Florus.

He left the cabin and headed for the town house. Two more days, and he'd be boarding a different ship. What lay at the end of that voyage, only time would tell.

Nearing Carthago, end of the voyage

Almost three weeks aboard a *corbita* with a master who'd tried to strangle him—Lusario had dreaded being trapped on the ninety-foot ship with a man who could do whatever he wanted with a slave. But Florus had mostly ignored him.

The arrogant young Roman who took such delight in showing who was master on land suffered from seasickness. When he wasn't in his room, Florus mostly leaned on the rail, pale as an elite maiden who avoided the sun and occasionally launching the last thing he ate into the sea.

With Florus staying near the cabin in the stern, all Lusario had to do was stay near the bow. He liked it there. The wind ruffled his hair, and spray from the waves slapping against the wooden planking dampened his face. When he licked his lips, he tasted salt.

If only their final port had been Apollonia, which served Cyrene like Portus served Rome. But they'd sailed past it without stopping.

Ships hugged the coast between Alexandria and Cyrene, so he'd never been out of sight of land. But from Cyrene to Carthago, they sailed across open water.

With nothing but sea and sky in all directions, even a free man might feel insignificant and vulnerable. As Florus's property, both were his reality, not just a feeling.

When the buildings of Carthago rose in the distance, Lusario's stomach turned as unsteady as his master's. But he swallowed his fear and squared his shoulders. Whatever lay ahead, he could bear it…at least for a while.

He jumped when something touched his back.

Famulus stepped up to the rail beside him. "The master wants to see you in his cabin." The corners of the valet's mouth were straight, and his eyes looked too sympathetic.

After being ignored for most of the trip, this sudden summons drove Lusario's heart rate from the pace of a plodding donkey to that of a galloping stallion.

"Did he say why?"

"No." Famulus rested his hand on Lusario's upper arm. "But he said not to come with you."

Lusario swallowed hard, but he willed his legs to carry him back to the cabin and Florus's closed door. He forced himself to take slow, deep breaths until his heart no longer raced. Then he knocked. What awaited behind those wooden planks couldn't be good, but when a master said come, there was no choice but to obey.

"Enter."

Lusario pushed the door open and stepped into the room. Eyes downcast, he clasped his hands. Florus sat on the edge of his bed, elbows on knees, forehead resting in his palms. Diokles had looked the same in the morning after many nights spent drinking too much wine with Florus.

As much as Lusario had enjoyed watching Florus fight seasickness for most of the trip, he masked his secret pleasure. "Can I do something for you, Master?"

When Florus lifted his head, his glare swept Lusario from head to sandals and back. The flush of anger replaced the pallor on his face. "It's what you better not do that you need to worry about. I gave Diokles the price of a minor houseslave or field worker, and that's what my father will think I bought. You'll be doing whatever kind of low-skill labor our steward assigns you. You are never to tell him you studied like a free man and thought yourself a scholar. If you even hint that you have the skills Diokles used to fool his father or that you took notes for me, I'll tell our steward you did something that will send you to the mines or the arena."

He stood and gripped the bunk-bed post to steady himself. But one hand was free, and he stepped forward to backhand Lusario's cheek. "You thought Achilleus would get you back to Cyrene with Diokles. Seeking his favor lost you mine. What you wanted didn't matter in Alexandria. What you want matters even less here. If you disobey me, I'll make sure you die slowly and in pain. Am I understood?"

Lusario bowed his head and stared at Florus's feet. "Yes, Master."

Florus placed his palm on Lusario's forehead and shoved him hard. "Get out of my sight."

Lusario stumbled backward, but he caught his balance and bowed before leaving the room. Despair wrapped around him, and he squeezed his eyes shut as he stepped out of the dimly lit cabin into the bright Carthaginian sun. He leaned against the rail and stared at the waves.

Maybe it would be better to climb over the edge and drop into the sea. The Romans thought suicide an honorable way to end a life that promised nothing but misery. They preferred the quick thrust of a dagger into their heart, but he had no access to a blade. If he didn't struggle, the ocean's deadly embrace would enfold him soon enough.

Both hands gripped the well-oiled wood, and his knees bent as he prepared to vault the rail and make the plunge.

He closed his eyes, and Timon's face appeared unbidden. "I'll be praying for God's best for you to come quickly. I don't know what that could be, but I'm certain it will come." As his friend's farewell words played in his mind, he froze. Timon always looked for the good in things, and he usually found some. He'd be saying it was too soon to despair when he didn't really know what lay ahead.

It was Florus's father, not Florus, who owned him. The steward would control what he actually did. He'd been a house slave before he became Diokles's valet. He could do it again while he waited for the right time to show he could do much more.

The harbor of Carthago

A seagull screamed overhead as the rowboats maneuvered the stern of the ship against the quay. Lusario leaned on the rail and watched as the gangplank was moved into place and the cover removed from the hold. Apollonia, Alexandria, Carthago—the bustle of a harbor seemed the same everywhere.

Famulus came to stand beside him. When Lusario glanced at him, he responded with a smile. "It's good to be home." His smile faded. "I'm sorry you couldn't go home, too, but the Florus town house is a better place to serve than many."

Lusario raised one eyebrow. What did Famulus expect him to say? From all he'd seen, being a Florus slave meant putting up with verbal insults and undeserved blows if the son of the household wasn't happy.

The valet peered up and down the quay, then bit his lip. "I thought someone would meet us. You did send a message with our ship and arrival date when you booked passage, didn't you?"

Send a message? Lusario sucked air between his teeth. "I didn't know I was supposed to. I was only told to book passage when I did the same for Diokles. He didn't have a message sent."

A glance toward the cabin, then Lusario touched the bruise on his cheek, avoiding the cut from Marcus Florus's signet. It wouldn't matter that he had no way to know he should have sent that message. But maybe Master Marcus didn't have to find out.

"How far is it to your house?"

"It's up past the forum in the Brysa district, where the elite townhouses are."

"Handcart distance or wagon?"

"A donkey cart should do it."

"The Alexandria harbor had places where you could rent them. And a sedan chair if Master Marcus isn't well enough to walk the distance. I would think the same is true here. I can get both if you have the money to pay for them."

Famulus eyed him. "If I tell you to go, and you don't come back…"

"I'll come back. You know what happens to runaways. I'd be a fool to risk that. Besides, I have nowhere to run."

He pushed back from the rail. "Get the baggage receipt from Master Marcus and make certain they bring everything up from the hold. We have two large trunks down there and a black chest that's mine. Plus the three chests under the bed in your room."

"You brought a chest?"

"A small one about the size of yours. It's mostly notes I took at the lectures." He massaged his neck. "Maybe I won't be allowed to keep them, but I thought it was worth trying. I couldn't leave them behind."

"I'll make sure it doesn't get left in the ship." Famulus flicked his hand toward the men securing the gangplank. "Go now. Maybe you can get what we need before Master Marcus realizes you had to do it because no one knows we're here."

Lusario trotted across the gangplank and headed toward the street between two warehouses fronting the quay. A donkey cart carrying several trunks came through the opening before he was halfway there. A few words with the man leading the donkey, and he'd arranged for him to come to their ship as soon as he unloaded his cargo. On the other side of the passage, he found two men with a sedan chair and led them back to await Marcus Florus's return to dry land.

"A denarius for the chair, two for the wagon." Whether either was a reasonable price, Lusario had no idea.

Famulus withdrew that sum from his purse and handed it to Lusario. Then he held out the baggage receipt. "I haven't seen our trunks yet. I need to help Master Marcus start home, but I'll stay with you to show you the way."

The first trunk came out of the hold, followed by the second. Lusario trotted over to intercept the men carrying them. He directed them toward the cart and resumed watching. Relief flooded him when his treasure chest of papyri and tablets appeared. He kept his eyes on the man who carried it to the cart and watched him slide it to the front alongside the big trunk.

After a few words with the crewman overseeing the dock slaves, Famulus took four from the line to follow him into the cabin. When they emerged with the two smaller chests balanced on their shoulders and the third carried by two men, Famulus pointed at Lusario, who raised his arm to summon them. As the three trudged toward the cart, Famulus returned to the cabin.

A toga-clad Marcus emerged, face pale but head high, and strode to the gangplank. Famulus walked close behind, arms held as if ready to catch Marcus if he faltered. With eyes fixed on the plank, Florus made it to the quay without any problem. Lusario stood motionless by the cart as Famulus held back the curtain of the sedan chair, and the man who hated him stepped in. The bearers stood and headed up the street that would take Florus home.

When Famulus waved at him, Lusario led the cart toward the passageway. Famulus fell in beside him, and the slow walk to whatever awaited began.

As they passed through the city, Famulus pointed out key landmarks: agora, baths, forum. They passed the forum atop the hill Famulus called the Brysa and went a few blocks farther.

Famulus turned to the donkey man. "We're here." When he knocked on the door, it swung open to reveal a small courtyard at the back of a town house.

The youth manning the door offered a broad smile. "Welcome

home, Famulus." He looked past to the cart. "I'll get help for the trunks."

He left the door open, and Famulus crossed his arms. "That's Canis."

With a forced smile, Lusario nodded. It was no surprise that people in Florus's household were named after what they did. So many door slaves were named as if they were dogs on guard. Would the steward let him keep his own name?

Three men came from the house and took the baggage out of the cart. Two grabbed the handles on either end of the first large trunk and bore it inside. The third hoisted Lusario's chest onto his shoulder.

He opened his mouth to claim his treasure box, but before he could speak, Famulus shook his head.

"That one and the other small one are mine. You can put them in my room." Famulus pointed at his own chest, and the house slave nodded before disappearing with the only thing of value Lusario had left.

"I share a room with Master Gaius's valet. I'll keep it safe for you." Famulus spoke so only Lusario would hear.

Lusario offered a grateful smile. "Thank you."

Famulus raised his hand in greeting as a middle-aged man strode toward him. "Steward Dromo." He lowered his voice. "Do all you're told quickly and as skillfully as you can, and it should go well for you here. Dromo is a fair man."

"Your master told me never to reveal what I'm trained for, so what should I say?"

"Tell Dromo you can do whatever he wants you to. Let him figure that out."

The smile Dromo directed toward Famulus was warm and welcoming. "It's good to see you back. You're looking much better than Master Marcus."

"Almost three weeks being seasick…it drains even a young man. I'm glad that's over for him."

Dromo's gaze shifted to Lusario, and his smile faded. "Who is this?"

"Lusario. Master Marcus won him gambling, so we brought him home."

"What's he good for?"

Famulus shrugged. "Whatever you want him to do."

"Hmph." Dromo flicked his hand toward the kitchen. "Report to the cook. He'll find something for you to do for now."

As Lusario headed where Dromo had pointed, he looked back over his shoulder. Famulus and Dromo stood with arms crossed, talking like old friends.

He blew out a long, slow breath. At least in the kitchen he didn't have to be at young Florus's beck and call. If Dromo was a good steward, like Famulus claimed, maybe, in time, life wouldn't feel so pointless.

Chapter 6

DREAMING BIG

The Martinus town house, Carthago, ten days later

Caelus Martinus stuck his head into the library, where his cousin Martina was curled up in her wicker chair, reading. "Good morning, cousin."

Martina lowered the scroll, and the welcoming smile he always got from her appeared. "You and Uncle Volero rode in early today."

"He's still at the estate. I came alone. Where's Grandfather?"

Her head drew back as if his solo arrival shocked her. But he was eighteen and a grown man, so why the surprise?

He'd dropped in on Grandfather for years, except that was usually in the afternoon when he finished doing something with friends. Since coming to live with Grandfather after her parents died six years ago, Martina usually saw him, too.

"He was still talking with Juliana when I finished breakfast."

It was no wonder Grandfather lingered over breakfast with his second wife. Juliana was a kind, smart woman who always made Caelus feel she was delighted to see him. When he was younger, it seemed strange that his mother disliked her and Martina so much. But when Grandfather told him the family secret a year ago and

43

made him promise never to tell his mother or sisters, what had been a mystery made perfect sense.

"Will he come here before the salutation?"

"He often does. But if he doesn't, he'll be in after everyone leaves." She rolled the scroll and stood to return it to the cubicle. "We could play *tabula* or *latrunculi* until he comes."

"I think I'll see if there are any honey rolls left." Caelus squeezed the back of his neck. "I need to talk to him before Father gets a chance to."

"Is it something I can help you with?" Her smile dimmed, and genuine concern shone in her eyes.

"Can you convince Grandfather that there's more to life than staying in Carthago and waiting for my turn to serve on the city council?"

"You don't want to stay here?" The smile had become a slight frown.

"I want more, and I know how to get it if Grandfather will just approve my plan."

She half-sat on the edge of Grandfather's desk. "What do you want to do?"

"I want to design villas and monuments. I want to build what I design and see people enjoying what I've made for them. I want to go to Alexandria and study with the architects and engineers who are the best in the world and then become one myself."

Martina followed each of his statements with a nod. "That doesn't seem unreasonable to me."

"It does to Father. That's why I want to talk to Grandfather, to convince him that I can do what no one before me in the family has done. If he says I can go, Father won't oppose him."

"I think you should try for your dream. Doing something only because everyone else says it's what you ought to do—that's not a good enough reason."

Caelus stepped into the library and closed the door. "I figured you'd understand. Both you and Juliana. I think I can persuade Grandfather, too. You're already seventeen, but you haven't been pestering him to find you a rich, handsome husband, like my sisters and their friends are all so eager for. So, you've shown him that some people need to make different choices than what's expected. He hasn't tried to force you to marry someone who doesn't share what you believe."

"No, but he's not happy that I've made the decision to follow Jesus like Juliana does, so don't use that as an argument for why you should be able to go to Alexandria. It might work against you, not for you."

"At least he wouldn't have to keep my plans a secret from almost everyone. He's wise to hide that you're a Christian from my mother and sisters. Sending me to Alexandria—that's something he could even brag about to his friends on the city council."

Martina pushed off from the desk and came to place a hand on his arm. "I'll be praying for you as you talk with him. Let me know what he says."

Caelus answered her offer with a nod. Like Father and Grandfather, he agreed with the Stoic philosopher Seneca's famous quote about those who believed in the gods, "Religion is regarded by the common people as true, by the wise as false, and by rulers as useful." He saw no reason to think faith in her god was any different.

But if believing the Christian teachings was why Martina was so kind and always looked for the best in everyone, then it was good that she did. His own sisters were just like his mother, who was jealous of the good things other people received and always found something to criticize.

But Mother's obsessive desire to outshine her female acquaintances, both friends and enemies, would serve his own goal well. She didn't care at all about him becoming an architect, but the prestige of him studying in Alexandria would give her something to brag about. She'd already told Father it would move him ahead of his peers on the road to greatness. How Father managed not to roll his eyes at Mother's desire for prominence among the elite was beyond comprehension sometimes.

He opened the door and stepped back into the peristyle. "Wish me luck. I need Fortuna to smile this morning."

Martina shook her head, but her caring smile remained. "Fortuna's not real, and you know it. So, she's not involved." Her voice was barely above a whisper. "But I will ask the One who controls what some call luck to give you success."

Caelus flashed her an appreciative smile and headed for the triclinium. He'd start by asking for a honey roll, but he'd end by sharing his big dream and asking Grandfather to make it come true.

When Caelus strolled into the triclinium, Grandfather and Juliana still reclined on the host's and center couches. He scooped up a rosemary-laced honey roll, inhaled its rich aroma, and took a bite. Then he sat on the couch opposite Grandfather.

Grandfather crumpled his napkin and dropped it on the table. "Why are you here so early? I wasn't expecting to see you until you and your father come for family dinner this evening."

"I wanted to talk about something vital to my future so you could be considering it before we dined later."

Grandfather swung his legs off the couch. "What would that be?"

Caelus drew a deep breath. Now that the time to ask was upon him, his stomach clenched. What if Grandfather thought it a stupid idea?

"I'd like to spend the final years of my studies learning something that might open a new business opportunity for the family."

Grandfather raised one eyebrow. "What would that be?"

"Between what you've taught me of Stoic philosophy and history and how well I've learned the oratorical skills needed for the council, I'm not sure another two years here in Carthago would add much to what I'll need to follow in Father's and your footsteps."

He cleared his throat. "But, if I went to Alexandria and studied with the best architects and engineers in the world, I could master the skills needed to start a business in Carthago as a designer and builder. No one here can teach me what I could learn there, and being trained by the best in the entire empire…that's going to appeal to anyone with the sense to appreciate that hiring an expert will give them something that will display both their taste and their wealth."

Grandfather stared at him, eyes narrowed, as he rubbed his chin. "What does your father think?"

Not the question Caelus wanted to hear. Father hadn't specifically said no, but he'd snorted as if he thought the idea absurd. Then he said that he saw no need for Caelus to travel to study something that probably wouldn't lead to what he expected. But if he repeated that, would Grandfather consider the matter settled?

Juliana sat up and offered Caelus the bowl that still held a few grapes. "It's an interesting idea. I can see how your mother and many other women who like to impress their friends would want something an Alexandria-trained designer could build for them."

Grandfather turned toward Juliana, and his brow furrowed. "Would you want such a thing?"

Juliana's light laugh triggered Grandfather's smile. "I'm not one to worry about what other elite women think of me, but if I were, I would definitely want to tell my friends I'd used a designer with the very best skills."

When Grandfather turned his gaze back on Caelus, behind those calculating eyes was the businessman weighing the possibilities.

"How long would it take?"

"As hard as I intend to work at it, I think I can learn everything I need in three years."

He wasn't sure he could, but asking for more time might lead to a no. When Grandfather saw how much he learned by then, surely he would extend the time, if needed.

As he rubbed his jaw, Grandfather frowned. But he also began to nod.

"That doesn't seem unreasonable for something that could create a new family business."

Juliana took a grape and slipped it between her lips. "Caelus has always been so diligent when you've been teaching him, so I'm certain he'll make us proud with this as well."

"I'm sure he will, too. I approve of you going to Alexandria. Your father can figure out the details for getting you there." Grandfather stood. "I'm meeting some of the council early to discuss a question about the harbor expansion. Then I'll be going to the baths. But I'll see you both at dinner."

He kissed Juliana on the cheek and strode from the room.

Caelus grinned at his step-grandmother. "Thank you."

She rose and rested her hand on his shoulder. "My pleasure. I'm sure you'll make the most of the opportunity, and I think God wants you in Alexandria for a while." She squeezed before removing her hand. "We'll miss seeing you often, but I feel this is something you're supposed to do."

"I'm certain of it." He gave her a quick hug before leaving the room to go find Martina. Whether his cousin's prayers had any effect or not, she deserved to be the first to know.

As Caelus entered the triclinium for dinner, he wiped his palms on his thighs. How would Grandfather reveal that he'd decided to let his grandson study in Alexandria without discussing it with Father first?

No one was reclining yet, and Caelus settled onto the right-hand couch where his cousin Martina would be joining him. Family dinner was always the same, with Grandfather and Juliana on the host's couch, Father on the center couch at the head of the table, and Caelus with Martina on the couch for the lowest ranked diners.

Martina entered and sat on the couch beside him. "Does Uncle Volero know what Grandfather decided yet?"

Caelus shook his head instead of answering. Father was striding along the peristyle toward the doorway. He'd be within earshot before Caelus could answer without Father hearing.

Martina patted his arm. "Grandfather will know the best way to tell him so he won't get too angry. I'll be praying." She kept her voice whisper-soft.

When Father passed through the doorway, he nodded a silent

greeting to Martina. He seldom spoke to her, although Caelus couldn't figure out why. Ever since he first met his cousin when he was twelve and she was eleven, he'd found her to be smart and kind and much better company than either of his sisters. Martina understood choosing an unconventional future and why following his dream to Alexandria was so important to him.

Mother hated Martina from the beginning because Grandfather favored the orphaned child of his favorite son over her own daughters, but even though Martina was a grown woman now, Father still mostly ignored her. Maybe being friendly with his niece wasn't worth having Mother fuss at him over it. Or maybe Father didn't like her being a Christian like Juliana and having to hide that from everyone but him, like Grandfather did.

Then Father raised an eyebrow at Caelus. "You left before breakfast, and I didn't see you at the baths with your friends."

"I spent most of the day with Sextus and Gaius. We watched some chariot races, then went to Sextus's house."

"Hmm." Volero settled onto the couch of honor. "Your grandfather expects you at family dinner, so it's good you left your friends to join us."

Out in the peristyle, the melodious voice of Juliana answered Grandfather's crisp words. Caelus's stomach clenched as they came nearer. When they stepped into the room, Grandfather's gaze shifted from his wife to his son." Good evening, Volero. I wasn't sure you'd be here yet."

Father rose and exchanged a quick embrace with Grandfather. "Felix is more readily persuaded while soaking at the baths than he ever is in the council chamber."

Grandfather sat on his couch and swung his legs up. After Juliana and the others joined him in reclining, the wine slave distributed the gold-lined silver goblets. As he poured the watered wine, another house slave slipped from the room to tell the kitchen they were ready to eat.

He returned with a tray carrying three small bowls of a white sauce and a tray of carrot sticks. After placing a bowl in front of each couch, he set the tray in the center where all could reach it.

"I think you're in for a delightful surprise." Juliana took a sip before setting her goblet on the table. "The spiced wine sauce for the carrots is something new that our underchef Colina created." She looked over her shoulder at Grandfather and received the smile Caelus usually saw him give her. "If you approve, dearest, it will be the appetizer at next week's banquet for the *duumvirs*."

Grandfather dipped a carrot in the bowl and bit off the sauce-coated end. "It's delicious. An excellent choice for that meal."

After he dipped again, he turned his gaze on Father. "Did you talk with Viator about which glassworks we might consider adding as a new business?"

"I tried." Father paused with his carrot stick just above the sauce. "He sailed for Rome yesterday to tend to some business there, but he's supposed to be back in Carthago in a month or so. His steward will let him know I called as soon as he returns."

Father lowered the carrot into the sauce, swirled it to get a thorough coating, and bit off the tip. "This is good. I'd like the recipe for my estate kitchen." He dipped the remaining carrot into the sauce. "Artoria has decided to collect glass sculptures, so adding a glassblowing shop to the family businesses will undoubtedly save me money."

"Adding a new business—that's something I've always enjoyed.

Caelus dropped in at the end of breakfast to propose one." Grandfather raised his goblet toward Caelus in a wordless toast. "It's good to see one so young already thinking about new business opportunities."

Volero raised an eyebrow. He cast a glance at Caelus, who looked down at the table. Father's eyebrow rising when paired with that slight frown always signaled his displeasure, and he hadn't even heard the proposal yet.

Caelus selected a carrot stick and dipped it in the sauce. But he didn't meet Father's eyes as he took a bite and dipped it again. Father's gaze returned to Grandfather. "A new business opportunity?"

"Our new design and construction business."

"From whom will you acquire that, Father?"

"We aren't buying it. We'll be sending Caelus to Alexandria to study for three years to gain the skills he needs to do the designs and to learn the best construction techniques."

Father directed a deeper frown toward Caelus. "Wouldn't it be less expensive to hire or buy someone with the skills to direct such an enterprise?"

"It might, but adding design and construction work to the family enterprises is Caelus's idea. I hadn't considered it before, but it has merit. It's only right that he develop the skills to oversee it. If he becomes good enough as an architect, he'll do much of the creative work himself."

Grandfather gave Caelus an approving smile. Father directed the opposite at him.

"Your brother was the adventurous one, always wanting to try something new. It looks like your son is much like his uncle. I'm pleased to see it. Caelus has always been smart and diligent when I was teaching him something. I'm sure he'll excel at this as well."

"I will agree that my son knows how to work a situation to his advantage." The edge on Father's voice made his statement criticism, not praise. Caelus stopped himself just before he bit his lip. Maybe making this maneuver to get past Father's objections had been fool-hardy.

Father rubbed his jaw. "We don't have any personal contacts that I know of in Alexandria. Sending one so young off to a major city knowing no one and virtually nothing about the area…I question whether it's wise for him to go to Alexandria without someone to help him get settled."

"Perhaps." Grandfather squeezed his lower lip. "But someone in the council should have the right contacts and be willing to help Caelus get started there. Make some inquiries to find someone who sent a son to Alexandria recently."

"Very well." Father's sigh was deeper than normal and directed straight at Caelus. "I'll begin looking for someone to guide how we'll get him moved and set up there."

Grandfather lifted his goblet toward Caelus. "To our future ar-chitect. I expect great things will come of this."

Juliana and Martina followed Grandfather's lead immediately. "To Caelus."

Father picked up his goblet, but he didn't raise it high. Still, when the three drank, he joined them in drinking the toast.

When Caelus dared to look at Father's face again, a wry smile greeted him. Father tipped his head, acknowledging Caelus's success in getting what he wanted most.

Caelus returned a smile of gratitude. It hadn't been Father's first choice for his future, but he was willing to help once Grandfather made the decision. If desire, dedication, and hard work meant anything, he would return from Alexandria as an architect who would make both the men he loved proud.

Chapter 7

Change for the Better

The Florus town house, two days later

Two weeks as a house slave in the Florus town house had convinced Lusario that serving there might be tolerable as long as Marcus Florus was still under his father's control. But he hadn't yet seen the eldest son who would become paterfamilias when the senior Florus died. Whether he'd be like his father or his brother…the uncertainty was enough to make Lusario's mouth go dry.

After working as an assistant tutor alongside his father and being a student of the finest teachers in the empire, scrubbing floors by hand with a wet rag chafed. But the senior Florus was entertaining some fellow members of the city council that evening, and Steward Dromo had decreed that everything would be spotless.

Lusario set the rhythm of strokes as he moved the rag forward and back, then let his mind focus on more meaningful things.

The philosophers he'd known in Alexandria were all free-born men. They had no idea what it was like to live as the property of another man.

Only one great philosopher had been born a slave. But Epictetus spent his youth as a slave of Epaphroditus, the freedman secretary of Emperor Nero. His owner had him study like a free man with the renowned equestrian Stoic, Musonius Rufus. Freed after Nero's death, Epictetus first taught in Rome and later started a famous school of philosophy in Nicopolis, the capital city of the Roman province of Epirus.

He taught that nothing external, neither death nor exile nor pain nor any such thing, can ever force a man to act against his will. But any menial slave knew Epictetus was dead wrong.

Except for his time in the lecture halls of Alexandria, Lusario had been forced many times to do what he didn't want to do. Since coming to Carthago, nothing he did from morning until night had been what he'd choose himself. For the farm slaves working the estates around Cyrene, pain and the fear of death made them act against their will every day until they died.

He'd finished what he could reach from where he knelt, so he moved to the left to reach the next section of the mosaic floor.

But under Roman law, male slaves weren't men. They were only *res mortales*, mortal things. Maybe that was how Epictetus could make that claim.

Master Philandros understood that the people he owned were still people. After becoming Marcus Florus's friend, Diokles had abandoned the humane ways of his father for the cold-blooded values of Rome.

As Lusario moved to the next dirty section, he stared at the rag in his hand. Once a man had a taste of what seemed like freedom, how could he be content with nothing more than the life of a menial slave?

He glanced over his shoulder when he heard footsteps. Marcus

Florus had entered the peristyle from the stableyard. As he strode across Lusario's freshly washed floor, he left a track of whatever it was he'd stepped on when he dismounted. It would need rewashing.

Lusario turned his face away. Maybe his enemy would walk by without noticing who wielded the washrag. But the hard slap on the back of his skull, followed by a kick to his side proved that hope was futile.

"You didn't clean it well enough, scholar. Do it better, or I'll get one of the whips from the stable. Then when I finish with you, you can clean up what I tracked in when I got it."

Marcus's chuckle followed him as he sauntered down the peristyle and climbed the stairs to the balcony, where he entered his bedchamber.

The deepest sigh drained Lusario's lungs. How long would his nemesis be up there? Was there time to clean up the muck he'd tracked in before he returned? Even if there was, would it make any difference?

With drooping shoulders, he picked up the pail and knelt by the first muddy footprint. Whether it would or not, he had to try.

The banquet for the councilmen was served in the larger triclinium overlooking the garden. Its three sets of three couches let the senior Florus entertain twenty-seven of the men he considered important in the highest style.

Lusario stood at the wall with two other slaves, waiting for the pause between appetizers and main course to slip in and clean both table and floor. With oysters on the half-shell among the offerings, there would be plenty of debris to gather off the floor mosaic of fishes. Plenty of other messes to wipe up as quickly as possible before the main course could be served.

At the snap of Steward Dromo's fingers, the shapely young women in too-short tunics moved forward to remove the used plates and platters. They slipped into the narrow spaces between couches and tables to take what was left of the appetizer course away. At the serving table along the wall, three men began cutting the meat for the main course into bite-sized pieces and distributing them among the silver plates embossed with scenes of gardens and gods.

No sooner had the girl stepped away from his table than Lusario moved in with a brass bucket embellished with a seascape. On hands and knees, he began to gather the empty shells and bread crusts that had been tossed on the floor by the diners as they ate.

He'd finished two sides when the man on the central couch close to Master Florus, a clean-shaven Roman old enough to be Diokles's father, cleared his throat.

"I heard your son has just returned from Alexandria, Gaius."

Master Florus held up his goblet, and the wine server came to fill it. "He has. Marcus spent two years studying there and returned two weeks ago."

"Then I'm in need of your advice."

"That's a twist, Volero. I'm usually seeking yours, and you never fail to give it." A trace of laughter colored Master Florus's voice. "It's even quite good…most of the time."

Volero chuckled. "I'm honored that you think so…mostly." He took a sip. "My son convinced Father that it would be advantageous for him to finish his education in Alexandria. Caelus is interested in architecture, and Father decided the practical things he would learn in that course of study would be better than merely restudying the Greek philosophy and history that he already taught his grandson."

Lusario glanced at the father of the would-be Alexandrian scholar. If only he belonged to that household.

Volero offered Master Florus a wry smile and a shrug. "But we have no contacts in that city. So, since your Marcus did what Caelus is planning, I'd like to know how you got him started there."

"A cousin of my wife was serving the Prefect of Egypt when he started. He arranged for lodging in a town house near the library and lecture halls and helped Marcus get settled." The master traced the rim of his goblet with his middle finger. "I can't offer her cousin's assistance to you since he's moved on to a different post in Syria. But I might have the perfect solution to your problem, anyway."

Lusario startled and looked up at the snap of his master's fingers. Master Florus flipped his upturned fingers to order Lusario to stand. Then he swept his hand toward Lusario.

"Marcus won a slave from one of his friends there and brought him home. He should know the city well enough to be of use to you."

The perfect solution? Lusario could hardly believe his ears. After one quick glance at the man called Volero, he stood with hands clasped, eyes downcast, waiting to be spoken to before he spoke. He erased all emotion from his face, but he couldn't keep his heart rate from rising. Escape from a life of drudgery and undeserved blows might be moments away.

Master Florus snapped his fingers again, and Lusario fixed a respectful gaze on him.

"Answer Martinus's questions truthfully so he can tell if he wants you."

"Yes, Master."

Could he risk telling the whole truth? He glanced at the third set of tables where Marcus had reclined with the youngest men. His enemy had already swung his legs off the couch, preparing to rise.

Martinus's eyes swept him from head to sandals and back. "Tell me what you know of Alexandria."

How much should he tell the man he hoped would become his new master? What would be enough to convince Martinus to buy him without getting him in deep trouble if Martinus decided not to?

"I can tell you about him." Marcus strolled over to stand behind his father's couch, arms crossed. "We've only owned him a month or so. His last owner was a Greek student from Cyrene, so he wasn't very particular about his attire. He used this one some as a valet. He was adequate, but he mostly did whatever menial tasks my friend needed." Marcus's nose twitched before he shrugged. "But, after two years in Alexandria, he is at least familiar with the parts of the city where scholars go and knows where to get laundry done."

The smile on the young master's face looked friendly enough. But the reptilian stare Marcus fixed on him renewed the promise of what would happen if Lusario dared to reveal what he'd really done for the two lazy sons.

Volero's glance at the young master accompanied a dismissive smile. Then his gaze locked on Lusario, and the smile vanished. Calculating eyes accompanied a frown. "What do you know of Alexandria?"

Lusario turned his eyes to meet Martinus's penetrating gaze. "I'm intimately familiar with the Greek quarter where the elite who come to study live and with the many places where scholars gather.

I know the harbor area, the forum, and the agora. As a province belonging to Emperor Hadrian, Aegyptus has many special rules, and I know how to keep that from becoming a problem. I speak Egyptian well enough that the locals understand me, and I can read and write the Demotic script used by ordinary Egyptians."

"Can you read and write Greek and Latin?"

"My father was a tutor in Cyrene, and he taught me."

"So, are you a scholar yourself?" Martinus's skeptical smile was fleeting, but genuine interest lit his eyes as he stroked his chin.

The young master cleared his throat. Mines or the arena…if Lusario said too much, either might be his next destination. But what did Martinus want to hear?

"I like to learn what I can. When I finished all my duties, I sometimes listened to lectures."

"A worthwhile use of your spare time." One corner of Martinus's mouth lifted. "My son, Caelus, is serious about learning all that he can while in Alexandria. He's convinced my father that three years there will make him an architect."

Martinus fingered his lower lip before he flicked his fingers to send Lusario back to cleaning.

As Lusario knelt to wipe up the dribbles of sauce by the end of the table, a carefully aimed grape hit his eye. With only the other eye open, he glanced at Marcus, who still stood behind his father's couch. As Marcus's eyes narrowed, he pulled a grape off the cluster in his hand, crushed it between thumb and forefinger, and flicked the mangled fruit into Lusario's cheek.

Lusario's stomach twisted. He'd said too much, and yet it wasn't enough to convince Martinus to buy him. How would Marcus deliver on his threat?

"Perfect might be too strong a word, Gaius, but he might be sufficient." Martinus traced the rim of his goblet before taking a sip. "Having a manservant who already knows Alexandria well should make my son's start there smoother. How much?"

"Seven hundred."

"That's rather high for a slave with no particular skills beyond knowing where things are in a city and speaking the local language. Perhaps six hundred fifty is more appropriate."

"Six hundred seventy-five and he's yours."

Martinus's eyebrows lowered, and he stroked his jaw. "That still seems high."

Lusario's heart pounded against his ribs. If only Martinus knew all he could do, he wouldn't be hesitating. Was it too late to tell him?

"But…" Martinus shrugged. "With someone who knows Alexandria looking after Caelus, perhaps Artoria won't be asking me at every meal whether I think our son is safe and doing well there. So, I'll take him."

As Martinus took another sip from his goblet, Lusario closed his eyes and released the breath he'd been holding.

Martinus set the goblet down. "My steward will come tomorrow to finalize the sale and bring him out to my estate. He can take over as manservant for Caelus until he leaves for Alexandria. A week should be enough to know if"—he pointed at Lusario—"your name?"

"Lusario, Master."

"If Lusario will be satisfactory."

Lusario clamped his jaw to keep the grin from escaping. He hadn't changed owners yet, and Marcus still might strike if he thought Lusario was too happy to have escaped his reach.

When he got back to Alexandria, Timon would be surprised by how quickly he'd exchanged a bad situation for a better one. Lusario didn't believe in any gods, but he wouldn't argue if Timon claimed that his prayers to his god deserved some credit. All that mattered was the result, not the cause.

No matter what Caelus Martinus was like, serving him was almost certainly going to be better than cleaning floors and carrying slop buckets. Escaping the malice of the lazy, lying son who felt threatened by what Lusario knew was best of all.

Chapter 8

More Than He Hoped For

The Florus town house, the next morning

Today—that could be early morning, late evening, or anything between. The uncertainty left Lusario's nerves stretched tight as a lyre string while he waited for the Martinus steward to claim him and get him out of the Florus house before Marcus struck.

He placed the last of the dirty plates and bowls on the tray before kneeling to wipe up a goblet's worth of wine where Marcus usually reclined.

One corner of his mouth curved. Why was he assuming Marcus would do something before he changed owners today? He hadn't said anything that should get Marcus's father asking about what Marcus had done that he shouldn't. Claiming he could write three languages was simply the truth. It didn't reveal he'd done the scholar's work that Marcus had claimed as his own.

But when Lusario began washing the floor as the final dinner guests left the room, Marcus had paused in the doorway. With eyebrows lowered and hand at waist level, he pointed at Lusario. Then keeping his hand close to his chest, he raised the pointed finger to his throat and drew it across. The final sneer before turning to follow the others triggered the same rise in his heart rate as Marcus finding him alone in a room.

Rag in hand, he was on his knees reaching for the spill when a shove sent him face-forward into the puddle. He rolled onto his back to find Marcus towering over him. Marcus put one foot on his chest and leaned most of his weight on it. Lusario fought the urge to jerk the foot and send Marcus tumbling. But he still belonged to Florus. Any attempt to defend himself could lead to a beating, a whipping, or worse, and Marcus would delight in taking his turn with the whip.

"Did you think you outmaneuvered me, scholar?" Marcus's voice was low and almost a hiss. He leaned further and gripped Lusario's jaw. "No one has paid for you yet. I can still do anything I want to you. And even after you're sold, whatever I do to you is only damaging property. Maybe I'll—"

"Master Marcus." Dromo's voice from the doorway made Marcus look over his shoulder. Then he slammed Lusario's head into the floor before releasing his chin and straightening. "What?"

"The bill of sale is signed, and the Martinus steward is here to claim their property."

A man of about fifty stood just behind Dromo. He stepped into the room. "Master Martinus bought a valet, not a footstool, and I'll be taking him now. I'd hate to have to tell our master how his new property was being mishandled. He might complain to your father."

Marcus lifted his foot, but he delivered a kick to Lusario's side before stepping away. "Take him. I'm through with him." He pushed past them and strode from the room.

Lusario rose and pulled the wine-soaked tunic away from his body.

"We'll get you a clean one before you go." Dromo held out his hand.

He pulled the tunic over his head and folded it before handing it to Dromo, who tossed it on the couch.

His chest of notes. It was in Famulus's room, but how could he reclaim it? Famulus could be anywhere in the house, and if Marcus knew he'd protected it for Lusario, the valet could be in trouble.

"I have a chest of writings I brought from Alexandria. Famulus has it in his room, but Master Marcus doesn't know."

A snort was Dromo's reply. "I wouldn't have told him, either. We'll stop there for you to get it on the way out."

"Thank you, Dromo." Lusario's grateful smile received a nod in return.

Dromo and the Martinus steward headed for the slave quarters. In only a few moments Lusario would follow his new steward out of his enemy's reach to a new life, dressed in a clean tunic and with his treasured notes on his shoulder.

Timon would have been pleased to know how quickly he'd found the way to something better than he'd expected.

The Martinus Estate, early afternoon

After about an hour, the mule team walked up to a villa, pulling the cart that held crates from the quay and Lusario, swinging his legs as he sat on the lowered tailgate. It continued past the decorative garden facing the road and around the back to the servant's entry.

Sedulus, the Martinus steward, climbed down from the driver's bench. "You'll be serving young Master Caelus as his valet until you leave for Alexandria and in whatever way he decides to use you when you get there. He knows you're coming, so after you get changed into the tunic worn by the personal slaves, you can wait in his room."

With a curve of his fingers, Sedulus called over the housemaid who was plucking dead flowers from the plants in a large urn by the portico. "Agatha, this is Lusario, Master Caelus's new valet. Show him where the young master's chamber is, then take him to get the right tunic."

Sedulus tapped the chest Lusario had balanced on his shoulder. "Leave this in his room until he decides what you should do with it."

"Yes, Steward Sedulus." Lusario dipped his head.

"You may address me as steward or Sedulus. You don't need both. Hard work and loyalty are rewarded in this household. I'll expect them from you at all times."

"Yes, steward."

After Sedulus strode into the peristyle and was out of earshot, Agatha offered a smile. "Steward spoke the truth. Master Volero is a good master, and so is Master Caelus. But…" She lowered her voice to a whisper. "You don't want to make Mistress Artoria or her daughters angry about anything."

Lusario nodded and whispered his reply. "I'll be careful. Thank you for warning me."

As he followed the girl into the house and up the stairs to the peristyle balcony, he drew a deep breath. So, even in this household there were people he'd have to placate to keep out of trouble. But at least he wasn't assigned to serve them, and they weren't starting out hating him.

Agatha stopped by a bedchamber that had a desk in front of the window and many codices and scrolls stacked in the cubicles of an open cabinet beside it.

"Put your box there." Agatha pointed to a spot by the cabinet. "I need to get back to the flowers before Mistress Artoria sees I'm missing. You can come back here after we get your tunic."

As Lusario followed her back onto the balcony, he glanced over his shoulder. His chest should fit under the bed. If he shoved it back against the wall, it wouldn't be obvious. Until he met Caelus Martinus and learned what kind of man he was, it was best if the tablets and papyrus sheets stayed where only he knew they were.

It took almost no time to change into the off-white tunic with blue edging around the armholes and neckline. With the clean Florus tunic folded under his arm, he climbed the balcony steps two at a time.

At the entrance to the bedchamber, Lusario froze. A handsome young man with wavy brown hair and a Roman nose stood looking through his chest. He held a stack of papyrus in one hand, reading the top sheet. Then he placed the papyrus back into the chest and took out a tablet. After scanning it, he stroked his jaw, as Lusario had seen his father do last night. Then a slow nod was followed by a crooked grin.

At Lusario's knock on the doorframe, Master Caelus's head jerked up, and he turned his gaze on Lusario, who still stood in the doorway.

Caelus tapped the open box with his foot. "This chest, is it yours?"

"Yes, Master."

Why hadn't he taken the moment he needed to hide it before he followed Agatha downstairs? If Marcus Florus had known he had it, he would have burned the contents piece by piece while Lusario watched, then made him clean up the ashes. Even after sneaking it onto the ship and hiding it in Famulus's room so Marcus wouldn't destroy it, was he about to lose the only thing of value he had left?

Caelus held up the tablet. "Who wrote this?"

Lusario squared his shoulders. "I did. Master Diokles had me go to lectures for him and write up what they taught."

"So he wouldn't have to do it himself, I'd wager." Caelus chuckled. "Did you do the same for Marcus Florus?"

Lusario fought the urge to bite his lip. He didn't belong to Florus anymore, but was there any risk left in revealing what young Florus had forbidden?

"Only for the last month or so. They were studying the same things."

"You mean you were studying and giving them something to send their fathers to make it appear they were doing what they should."

Lusario dropped his gaze to the floor. "Yes, mostly." He glanced up at Caelus. "Master Marcus was smart enough to do it himself. Master Diokles…he needed some help."

Caelus tapped the closed tablet on his palm. "This analysis of the arguments between the Stoic and the Epicurean…it's very good. As good as I could have done myself. You'll find that I take my studies very seriously. I won't be asking you to do the work I should. Besides, I would never lie to my father like that. No man should."

Lusario bit his lip. "I didn't mind doing it for Master Diokles.

My father tutored him as a boy. I'd already started assisting in the school Master Philandros owned when he made me his son's valet to watch over him in Alexandria."

One corner of Caelus's mouth curved into a wry smile. "My father bought you to watch over me in Alexandria. When it comes to scholarly matters, I don't need anyone's help. But, frankly, I think you watching over me is a good idea. Serve me well, and you can use your spare time to add more notes to your collection."

Caelus set the tablet back in the chest. "Our family knows very little about Egypt and nothing about Alexandria. I've read what Herodotus wrote about it, but that was before the Ptolemies, so much would have changed. Of course, I've also read what Polybius wrote about Egypt, but that was almost 300 years ago when it was still under Greek rule."

He shrugged. "I just reread what Strabo wrote about the province under Roman rule. He includes a lengthy description of Alexandria. But even that is a hundred years ago, and there must have been some changes."

With one eyebrow raised, he contemplated Lusario. "Have you read any of these?"

"I have." Lusario kept his smile subdued, but he couldn't stop it completely. Returning to Alexandria, serving a true scholar…he couldn't ask for much more. "What Strabo wrote is still mostly true."

"What about Plinius's Natural History? Have you read that?"

"Yes, and works by the best historians and philosophers. The Great Library is open to all."

Caelus's eyes narrowed, and he fingered his lip, just as his father had done. "What about Thales and Pythagoras?"

"I've studied geometry, too."

"Are you good at it?"

Lusario squared his shoulders. Caelus seemed like a master who wanted the truth, not fake humility. "I am."

Caelus slapped his thigh. "I'd be willing to wager Marcus's father had no idea what his son brought home from Alexandria, or he would never have sold you to Father for the price of a house slave."

"He didn't. Master Marcus told me I'd be in the mines if I let his father know I'd done more than dress Diokles and run errands."

"Well, my father is going to find it highly amusing when I tell him. He always pays a fair price, but he likes a good bargain."

Caelus crossed his arms. "I'm not going to let you pick random lectures to attend."

Lusario's mouth drooped before he thought to stop it. No more lectures—Marcus Florus would be laughing if he knew. But would his new master at least let him read at the library?

"Don't look so disappointed. The lectures you go to won't be random. You'll be coming with me to the ones I attend." His foot nudged the chest. "You'll take notes like you did before. You're going to learn what I'm learning so you can be my assistant when I start designing and building in the new family business I promised Grandfather I could start. If all goes well, you might earn your freedom and continue working with me as a freedman."

He picked up the tablet and scanned it again. "I can't guarantee that, but Grandfather knows value and rewards those who serve him well." He snapped the tablet shut. "But at the very least, I can guarantee you'll find life more interesting than you ever have before."

Lusario didn't even try to stop the grin. "I'll do all I can to serve you well, Master."

Caelus slapped his arm. "I'm sure you will. But Father planned on you being my valet, too, and I'll be joining some of his friends at dinner tonight. They're councilmen, so it will be togas."

Lusario straightened. "I've only served Greeks who weren't citizens."

"So, you've never wrapped a toga." Caelus opened a trunk, took out a folded toga, and handed it to Lusario. "Father's valet, Terio, can teach you."

He returned the tablet to the chest and closed the lid. "You'll be sleeping in the slave quarters, but this will stay here for safekeeping until we go to Alexandria. We'll find Terio now, and he'll show you what you need to do."

"Yes, Master Caelus."

Caelus glanced over his shoulder as he strode toward the door. "When it's just the two of us, you can drop the 'master.' Caelus is enough when no one else is listening."

As Lusario followed his new master onto the balcony, he couldn't stop shaking his head. From the threat of death for revealing what he knew to a seat near his new master in the lecture halls of Alexandria as they became engineers—who would have thought a night of drunken gambling could lead to even more than he'd ever hoped for?

Chapter 9

THE RIGHT MAN TO TRUST

A road south of Carthago, 4 days later

Lusario relaxed in the saddle as he reined the gelding from a canter back to a walk. If anyone had told him in Cyrene that his duties as valet would include racing across the countryside while his master rode a spirited stallion next to him, he would have thought them crazy. But he'd spent the last two days learning to ride well enough to go as fast as Caelus Martinus wanted.

The thunder of hooves, the rhythm of moving with the horse, the wind in his face like he'd felt on the ship—it was no wonder Caelus said nothing both exhilarated and relaxed him like a good ride.

They'd ridden south from the estate and deeper into the countryside, passing vineyards, olive groves, and fields of wheat that rippled in the breeze. Everywhere he looked, the future food of the imperial city lay before him.

Caelus's grandfather had planned a banquet with a few close friends to send the future architect off to Alexandria for three years. It was time to return to the villa to gather the toga and fine-linen tunic before following his young master to the town house, where

Lusario would do his first toga wrap when the elegance of the drap-
ing mattered.

The stallion tossed its head and shook its mane before stretching
its neck to pull on the reins.

"Steady, Zephyr. I know you'd rather run than walk, but I need
to talk awhile."

He shifted in the saddle to look at Lusario. "While we're in Alexandria, I plan to visit many of the nearby monuments. There must
be quite a few built by the ancients, but I'm most interested in the
newer ones built by several of the emperors. We'll need to buy a
couple of good horses for that."

Lusario rubbed his jaw. "None of the young men where my last
masters lived had their own horses. Not that I knew of, anyway.
There was no stable at the town house. But it wasn't far to the harbor, and there were stables that rented horses to people who came
in on the ships."

Caelus patted his stallion's neck. "Horses as good as this one?"

"More like this one. There are so many canals connecting towns
in the delta that people mostly travel by boat. But I can try to find
one that rents quality horses for you. Egyptians use donkeys more
often than horses. If we go somewhere by boat, we can probably
rent those where we land."

"That wouldn't be my first choice." Caelus wrinkled his nose,
then shrugged. "But if there aren't horses, maybe there will be mules.
Or you can find someone where I can board some good horses for
when I want them."

"Perhaps. The horses that race at the hippodrome just east of
town must stay somewhere nearby. I can ask there."

Caelus flexed his calves, and the stallion resumed the distance-swallowing trot that seemed to be the young master's favorite speed. Lusario nudged his gelding and settled in next to the master who'd told him to ride beside, not behind him, whenever there was room.

As they passed the edge of an olive grove that blocked the view of the road ahead, two men on horseback came toward them. One rode a high-stepping stallion; the other sat astride a gelding that plodded along.

Lusario stiffened. "That's Marcus Florus." Even though he belonged to Martinus now, the venom in Florus's eyes as he delivered his final kick promised that his threat would not be soon forgotten. Under Roman law, anything Florus did to him was only property damage.

When the man on the stallion raised a hand in greeting, Caelus slowed to a walk. "The one on the stallion is Gaius Lupulus. His family estate is south of ours. We studied with the same rhetor when I started learning oratory. He's a couple of years older than me and a good man, from all I ever saw." His nose twitched. "Why he chooses Florus for a companion…"

A wordless nod was Lusario's wisest response. He would have said Diokles would grow into a good man before Florus got his hooks into him. But with his first young master back in Cyrene and Florus no longer beside him, maybe he'd still become a good man like his father.

When they drew abreast on the road, Lupulus reined in. "*Salve*, Martinus. I didn't expect to see you here. I heard you'd left for Alexandria."

"I'm leaving in a few days. The second cousin of one of the duumvirs will be arranging lodging for me in the Greek quarter this week." Caelus pointed at Lusario. "Lusario knows the city well, and he recommended several town houses near the library and lecture halls where Roman students rent lodgings. Paternus's cousin will have rented something for me before I get there."

Florus's glare raked Lusario before he snorted. "Only a fool takes a Cyrenian slave's word for anything."

"That depends entirely on the slave, whether Cyrenian or not. But I could say the same for free men." The stallion fidgeted, and Caelus leaned over to pat its neck. "I was just reading an insightful analysis of an argument in Alexandria a couple of months ago between a Stoic and an Epicurean. I can send you a copy, if you like." He straightened in the saddle and fixed his gaze on Florus. "Or perhaps your father would enjoy it, if he hasn't already seen it. My father did, especially when he learned who really wrote it."

Florus's knuckles whitened as his grip on the reins tightened. His frown deepened into a scowl, but his blinks came too quickly. Was that fear of what his father would do if Volero Martinus told him or anger that Master Caelus knew what he'd done and had the gall to tease him about it?

One corner of Caelus's mouth lifted. "As a Stoic myself, I tend to agree with Seneca on most things, including how to judge the worth of a man and decide who deserves my consideration."

Caelus squared his shoulders and raised a hand as if he addressed an assembly. 'I shall choose an honest, plain man, with a good memory and grateful for kindness; one who keeps his hands off other men's goods, yet does not greedily hold to his own, and who is kind to others. When I have chosen such a man, I shall have acted, to my mind, although fortune may have bestowed upon him no means of returning my kindness.' Perhaps I owe you my thanks for bringing such a man from Alexandria for me."

Florus flushed deepest red, but it was anger, not embarrassment. Lusario had seen that shade before, and it was always followed by a blow to his head. But this time only a torrent of curses assaulted his ears.

Lupulus's eyes widened, and he stared at Florus. When he turned his gaze back to Caelus, he faked a chuckle. "Since you've only owned this one for a week and Marcus saw him with his old owner for nearly two years before winning him, I wonder that you think yourself the better judge of what your father bought." He shrugged. "If he's not what you think…" Lupulus sucked air through his teeth. "I guess you'll find that out the hard way when you're too far from home to do anything about it."

After a glance at Florus, Lupulus turned his social smile toward Caelus. "Father is expecting me, so I must be going. I wish you a safe voyage and a productive time in Alexandria with your Cyrenian slave." His next chuckle sounded genuine enough. "You can tell us in three years whether you chose wisely about whom you decided to trust."

As the two riders headed south, Caelus started them north again.

Lusario cleared his throat. "I will always try to be that kind of man as I serve you, Master Caelus."

"That's what I'm expecting. Father will be waiting for us, so we need to hurry. He doesn't like to be late, and neither do I." Caelus tapped Lusario's arm with the back of his hand, then urged his horse into a trot.

As Lusario followed, it was all he could do to stop the grin.

Timon had wished he had a master as good as Achilleus. If he were a betting man, it would be safe to bet that he did.

Alexandria, four weeks later

The sun was halfway to the horizon, and Lusario stood beside Caelus at the ship's rail. In silence, they watched the rowboats maneuver their ship in Eunostos Harbor, the western harbor that handled much of Alexandria's commercial shipping. At ninety feet in length, the corbita they'd taken from Carthago was only half as long as the largest grain ship they passed as they moved along the quay to an open berth.

Caelus leaned on the railing. "I'm sorry our ship didn't go into the Great Harbor so we'd sail past the Pharos lighthouse." He rubbed his jaw. "Strabo said that lighthouse is faced with white marble. When the sun hits it right, it should be stunning."

He straightened and crossed his arms. "I can see why they call the Pharos one of the seven great wonders of the world. Plinius wrote that Sostratus of Cnidus designed it for the first Ptolemy to show mariners where the safe entrance to the harbor was. To design and build something like that…" He nudged Lusario. "We'll probably never do anything that grand, but only time will tell."

Lusario stopped the wry smile before Caelus saw it. He had no illusions that he'd ever do anything that would draw people from across the empire to see it, but it would be enough to build something that the people who paid for it would enjoy.

"After we get settled in your lodgings, we can visit it." Lusario pointed at the causeway that lay to the east, connecting the main city to Pharos Island. "It's an easy walk across the Heptastadium. It separates the Enostos from the Great Harbor, but two bridges let smaller ships pass between them. We can go to the base of the lighthouse, and you can probably go inside and look out from one of the rooms on the fourth floor."

"Will they let us climb to the top where the fire burns at night?"

"We can ask." Lusario shrugged. "It's over three hundred feet to the top. I wouldn't want to be the one carrying the oil up the stairs to feed the flame each night."

Stern first, the ship was pulled into its berth and the gangplank lowered.

"Now what?" Caelus massaged the back of his neck.

"We collect our baggage and take it to the house of the duumvir's cousin."

Caelus lowered his hand and rested it on the handle of his dagger. "I know the address of the town house of Paternus's cousin. Is that enough to get us there?"

"I can find anything in the city if I know its address." Lusario swept his hand toward the cabin, inviting Caelus to go ahead of him. "But after we get the trunks, we have to pass through customs. It's illegal to use regular Roman coins in this province. It's a policy left over from when the Ptolemies ruled. The customs men will look in every case to make sure we aren't trying to smuggle any in. After we get the coins you brought exchanged for Alexandrian ones, we can pay porters to carry the baggage to the house, or maybe hire a handcart."

"The first of many special rules for Egypt?"

"Yes."

"Father bought you to keep my mother from fretting all the time about whether I'm safe so far from home. Some peace at dinnertime was worth your cost to him." Caelus's wry smile accompanied laughing eyes. "But it would have been money well spent just to have you looking out for things like this."

"I'll do my best to make it so."

Lusario kept his gaze on his young master's back as they strolled to the cabin. It felt good to be valued, even for the smallest things.

Caelus glanced over his shoulder. "Our host can tell us where to take the letter of credit tomorrow. Father gave me the name of the bank here that handles such things for the bank he uses in Carthago. I suppose they'll take care of changing the balance from denarii to drachmas."

"When I did that for Diokles, the bank his father used took care of it."

They passed through the cabin doorway and entered the room they'd shared for the past three weeks. From beneath the lower bunk, Lusario pulled out two large and one mid-sized chest. The first two held Caelus's toga, the rest of their clothes, and other personal items. The other held the scrolls and codices Caelus decided to bring. From the foot of his upper bunk bed, he collected his own small chest of treasured notes and tablets.

"I'll be writing Father tonight to let him know we made it without any problems and where I'll be living. Then he can tell Mother not to fret about how I'll be doing because your knowledge of Egypt's special rules has helped already." One corner of Caelus's mouth lifted. "Perhaps I should write to Lupulus, too, to tell him it's already obvious I chose to trust the right man."

Lusario didn't even try to stop the smile. Serving someone who appreciated even little things—that was the last thing he expected when he exchanged Florus's Alexandrian drachmas for Roman denarii before they left Egypt.

Exchanging his first Roman master for his current one…that had been the best thing that ever happened to him.

Chapter 10

New Home, New Goals

The Regillus town house

The sun was a blazing orb half-hidden at the edge of the sea. The bank of clouds whose underside it painted orange hovered above it. Too soon the long shadows its rays still formed would disappear when the sun slipped below the horizon.

When the sun's rays vanished, those who loved darkness began to stir.

Lusario massaged the back of his neck. In a city the size of Alexandria, darkness often meant danger. Caelus looked like a man who'd have something worth stealing. They needed to get off the streets soon.

It had taken too long getting through customs. He'd chosen the wrong line. What looked like only one trunk ahead of them turned into two dozen more when a merchant's slaves joined him. But at least he'd managed to hire the last handcart for Caelus's two trunks and chest, and the duumvir's cousin lived to the west of the Great Library instead of the eastern edge of the Greek Quarter, next to what had been the Jewish Quarter of the city.

His own small chest rested on his shoulder as he led Caelus and their baggage the final block to the address they had for their host.

At the door, he lowered the chest to his feet and knocked. It was only moments until the door swung in, and a youth stood staring at them.

Lusario cleared his throat. "Caelus Publilius Martinus to see Aemelius Regillus. Your master is expecting him."

Behind the youth, a man about the age of Martinus's steward strode toward them. "Master Regillus expected you a few hours ago. With the sun almost down, I was becoming concerned." He swept his hand toward the atrium. "Come in."

He turned to the door slave. "Get two men to bring in their baggage."

As the youth scurried toward the back of the house, Caelus stepped past Lusario. "The ship was late arriving, and unfortunately we were behind a merchant in customs who had many trunks that the agents thought needed careful examination."

Lusario stayed in the open doorway, watching the street as he waited for the house slaves. He pointed to the mosaic of the growling dog in the entryway. "You can unload everything here."

He'd paid at the docks for the use of the cart, but he took two bronze chalkons, the smallest Alexandrian coin, from his purse and gave one to each of the men who'd done the real work. The weariness vanished from both faces, and they muttered their thanks before turning the cart around and heading back to the harbor.

As he watched them, two large men appeared beside him. With one on each end of the largest trunk, they carried it up to the atrium balcony and disappeared into a bedchamber. Two more trips took the second trunk and Caelus's chest up the stairs, and Lusario followed behind with his treasure box.

Caelus stood in the atrium with the steward. "Lusario, come here when you get that put away."

Lusario set his chest by the bed before trotting down the stairs to stand behind Caelus.

"Repeat what you just told me. I want Lusario to hear it as well. He'll be taking care of many details for me."

"I've rented you a large chamber at the Latinus town house east of the gymnasium."

Caelus raised his eyebrows at Lusario. "Do you know it?"

Did he know it? It was where Diokles and Florus had lived for two years. He'd be dining with his friends among the servants again. "Yes, Master Caelus."

Regillus's steward's eyebrows dipped. "You do?"

"Is it close enough for us to visit this evening?" Caelus directed a hopeful smile at Lusario.

Before he could answer, the steward raised a hand to stop them. "Now is not the time for you to be strolling around the city without a guard, even if your man does know where that house is. Master Regillus plans to dine with you shortly to hear news of the city where he spent some of his childhood."

"Does your master prefer to dine in toga?"

The steward's mouth twitched. "When he doesn't have important guests, he doesn't wear one himself. You can do as you wish."

In Caelus's quick glance, Lusario saw the silent laughter. "I shall follow his lead. Please send someone for me when he's ready."

"Of course. First, I'll send someone with some cleansing oils and water so you can clean up before dinner." With a tip of his head, the steward turned and headed into the peristyle.

Caelus led them up to the room. He signaled for Lusario to close the door before he sat and flopped back on the bed. "I'm only here for one night as a favor to a second cousin. I have no illusion of importance in our host's eyes, but I'll try to make his dinner with a young stranger as entertaining as possible. Not having to figure out where to stay myself…that's worth my effort and gratitude."

He sat up. "Perhaps he'll have interesting things to tell me about Alexandria, too. Father always says a few well-chosen questions to show your interest can turn a stranger into a friendly acquaintance before the conversation's done."

Three knocks announced the arrival of oil, water, and towels, and Lusario opened the door. As the housemaid placed the basin, pitcher, and other items on the side table, Caelus stood. "Find out where my valet will be eating, and have someone get him when I go down to dine."

The girl nodded, bowed, and left.

As Caelus pulled the tunic over his head, Lusario opened the trunk to get a *strigil*. Then he used it to scrape off the oil he applied to Caelus to remove any dirt and sweat.

He'd barely finished when a youth summoned them both to their dinners.

As Caelus turned into the triclinium and was greeted by the master of the house, Lusario went on to the slaves' dining area. As he stepped into the room and was directed to a seat, he worked at stopping a grin.

Tomorrow, he'd once again see the halls and porticos of the

greatest library in the world, maybe sit in the back of a lecture hall while an expert taught something he'd never heard before.

Had Achilleus returned from the visit to his grandfather's estate? What would Timon say when he learned what seemed certain to end with him dying in the mines had instead placed him on the path to becoming a freedman engineer?

He ate his first mouthful of the lentil stew, and his head drew back. The savory flavor of turnips, leeks, celery, coriander, and garlic burst across his tongue. It was even better than what Martinus fed his people.

The food for servants and slaves at the Latinus town house had been edible, and there was always plenty of it. If they moved from their host's house to their permanent lodgings before dinner tomorrow, he wouldn't be eating as well. But that humble dinner would satisfy far better than the finest banquet, for he would dine once more with old friends.

The next morning

Lusario stood by their chamber window, watching ships move in and out of the harbors as he waited for Caelus to come from breakfast with their host. The toga lay on the bed, ready to wrap. It would declare Caelus's status as a Roman citizen when they went to the library and lecture halls. On the rare occasions when Florus attended a lecture, Famulus always dressed him to flaunt his citizenship. In this city with its rigid hierarchy of Romans over Alexandrians over all other Egyptians, Florus made the most of his privileges.

Faint words reached him as Caelus bid his host a good morning before climbing the stairs.

"Regillus just told me to be sure to call upon him if I run into any problems here that prove too difficult for me to deal with. If Father ever visits, I must introduce him to Regillus. I think they would both enjoy the acquaintance." Caelus strolled to the bed and fingered the toga. "For my first exploration of the city, I'll leave the toga here. I want to blend in, not stand out today."

"As you wish." Lusario's mouth twitched. Togas were a nuisance, whether you were the wearer or the wrapper. Anytime Caelus didn't want his was fine with him.

Caelus rummaged in the larger trunk and withdrew a wooden sheath with brass overlays. He pulled out the dagger and felt the edge of the blade. "Father sent this with me, but should I wear it or not?"

Lusario's brow furrowed. He'd never seen Caelus wear one before. "Do you know how to use it well?"

The chuckle made Lusario draw his head back.

"I've never had occasion to use it at all. I didn't wear one in Carthago."

"If you're not alone, I think it's safe enough here without one, at least in the daytime. I never felt unsafe, but I didn't look worth robbing. Florus and Diokles went many places during the day without one. I don't know what Florus did at night."

His sadistic master always used hand or foot to strike. Would he have chosen a cut over a bruise if he had a dagger handy?

Caelus returned it to the trunk. "Something to ask the steward of the Latinus town house today. He should know what his lodgers do."

He led them downstairs and headed toward the front door. They had just reached the vestibulum when—

"Martinus."

They turned to find the steward striding toward them. "Master Regillus thought it wise to provide someone to guide you today. Many in the city speak no Latin, and some know very little Greek. And there are those who would misdirect you for amusement or worse."

"Thank him for the offer, but my manservant lived in this city for two years. He's very familiar with all the places we'll be visiting today and speaks Egyptian as well as Latin and Greek. We're going to the Great Library first, then on to the Latinus town house. After I determine exactly where I'll be staying, Lusario will return to arrange the delivery of our baggage."

A tip of the steward's head accompanied a fleeting smile. "As you wish, but it is wise to be off the streets before dark." His gaze scanned Lusario from sandals to hair and back. "But your valet should already have advised you of the wisdom of that."

"I'll keep Master Caelus away from danger." He glanced toward their bedchamber. "Master has a dagger that I can carry, if you think it wise."

A corner of Caelus's mouth lifted, as if he thought that offer amusing. But Lusario would do anything to keep from changing masters again. He had too much to lose.

"I'll make sure I'm inside either here or at our lodgings before dark. Thank Regillus for his kind concern."

Caelus led them into the street. "Where now?"

"East up Canopic Street will take us to the Great Library."

"Lead on."

Caelus fell in beside him as Lusario headed toward the complex of public buildings where he'd known his greatest happiness.

The first one stood to their left. "You'll hear that called the Mouseion in Greek or the Museum in Latin. It was built by the first Ptolemy as a shrine for the Muses. It housed the start of the library." As they walked past it, he pointed to the connecting building. "Just to the north is the Great Library itself, built by the second Ptolemy. Its collection holds hundreds of thousands of scrolls and codices."

Caelus stared at him. "How does anyone find the scrolls they're looking for?"

"Librarians get them for you, and you use them in the reading room. They don't allow any of the collection to leave the building."

Lusario pointed east across the garden. "Over there are the lecture halls. Where those people are gathered is where they post the schedule for the next few days."

Caelus lengthened his stride, and Lusario hurried to keep up with his taller master. With arms crossed, Caelus read the list of lectures.

"There are several that look useful. Several more that look interesting." He rubbed the back of his neck. "I need to find someone who can tell us what we need to be studying and where to start. Three years might seem like a lot of time, but I don't want to waste any of it in case Grandfather decides those three years are all I have here."

As Lusario joined Caelus in scanning the choices, a familiar voice came from behind.

"Lusario?"

As he turned, Lusario felt his smile grow. Timon trotted toward him, wearing the biggest grin Lusario had seen on him yet. He took a few steps toward his approaching friend.

"I thought that was you, but it seemed impossible to be so. I thought something good might happen, but seeing you back here…"

"I changed masters in Carthago. I'm serving Caelus Publilius Martinus now."

Caelus turned at his name. "An old friend, Lusario?"

"A good friend, Master Caelus."

Caelus glanced at Timon, then turned his gaze back on Lusario. "I'm going to see what's inside the main library. You can talk to your friend for a while. Come find me when you're through."

"Yes, Master."

Caelus strode toward the main entrance to the library, and Lusario pointed at the bench where he'd shared his devastating loss with Timon only two months ago. It was fitting to share his future plans on the same bench with the man whose parting words had kept him from dying before hope could be reborn.

Chapter 11

How Things Change

As soon as they settled onto the cool stone of the shadowed bench, Lusario turned to face Timon. "I have you to thank for me being here."

His friend's eyes narrowed. "What did I do?"

"You came to say goodbye. If you hadn't, I'd be dead now."

Timon's eyes saucered as his head drew back, and Lusario's chuckle narrowed his friend's eyes again.

"Maybe you don't remember what you said, but I'll never forget it."

Lusario shifted his gaze to the library across the garden. Some things were easier spoken without looking at the man you talked to.

"Florus spent the whole voyage seasick, so he never left the cabin or the rail beside it. I avoided him the whole trip." Lusario grinned. It still gave him pleasure to think about how miserable Florus had been. It was the least he deserved.

"But as we approached Carthago's harbor, he sent Famulus for me. He said the price he paid would make his father think I was some low-skill house slave, and that was what I would always be in his household. He told me he hated Achilleus, and because your master tried to help me, he would make my life as miserable as he could. I was never to tell anyone I did more than help Diokles dress and run errands for him. He would tell the steward something that would send me to the mines or the arena if I did."

With his thumb, Lusario massaged his palm. "After studying as if I were a free man here, the expectation of nothing more than what he said…well, I decided if I was going to die, I would choose when and how. I was about to jump the rail and drown when I remembered your final words."

"What did I say?"

"You'd be praying for your god's best to come quickly. You didn't know what that would be, but you were certain it would come." Lusario glanced at his friend, then returned his gaze to the garden. "You always looked for the good in things, and you usually found some. I knew you would tell me it was too soon to despair when I really didn't know what lay ahead."

He switched the hand he massaged. "So, I decided to wait to see if you were right. Maybe Florus's father was better than his son. The steward really decides what the house slaves do, and maybe he'd see I could do so much more without me saying a word. Then what Marcus said wouldn't matter."

He faced Timon with a smile. "You were right. Within two weeks, his father suggested Volero Martinus buy me to help his son Caelus get started well in Alexandria." He tipped his head toward the library, where Caelus would be figuring out what they'd do next. "Caelus plans for me to study engineering with him. He wants me to work with him starting a design and construction business when we finish. I used to envy you having Achilleus as master, but Caelus is just as good."

As Lusario talked, Timon's smile kept broadening. "Master

Achilleus will be as glad as I am to hear this when he gets out of the lecture. Clear answers to prayer are always cause for rejoicing."

Lusario's mouth twitched. "It was your words that encouraged me to hold off until I knew my fate. Whether your god had anything to do with it…that's not something we can know."

Out of respect for his friend's feelings, he refrained from saying that no god was real so they never did something about anything.

"Sometimes we can know for certain." Timon scanned the area around them, then leaned toward him. "After I confessed that Jesus was my Lord and Savior, God's Spirit came to dwell within me. Sometimes the Spirit tells a Christian something directly."

Lusario suppressed a chuckle and fought to keep the incredulity off his face. "Tells you directly? Some people claim to be oracles who hear messages from their god, but I doubt that. From all I've seen, the gods are only stories passed down from our ancestors, not real beings with power. Their priests and oracles make a good living from the offerings of the superstitious. Surely you're familiar with how Seneca explained the role of religion."

Timon shrugged, but his smile didn't waver. "I know he said that religion is regarded by the common people as true, by the wise as false, and by rulers as useful. But I'm not talking about religion. I'm talking about the one true God, the God with real power who created everything we see around us, not an ancient story made up by the ancestors. He doesn't want endless repetition of formal prayers where the slightest deviation from the rite means you have to start over. The Romans don't care what you believe as long as you perform their rites correctly. God cares what you truly believe."

He turned and rested his thigh and knee on the bench to face Lusario directly. "That's the God we worship. When we pray to him, it's like talking with a person. He listens and responds." His lips straightened as his eyes turned serious. "He's the only god worth following."

Lusario tightened his lips and shook his head. "Master Caelus is a Stoic, and his father and grandfather have been committed Stoics since their youth. I'm not going to follow a so-called god who could lose me what I'm going to become as I study with Caelus."

"Truth has value in itself, and Jesus told his followers that He is the Way, the Truth, and the Life."

How could a man claim to be *the* truth? Truth was the opposite of falsehood, not something a person could be.

"It does, but it doesn't make sense for a man to be calling himself the truth. He could be truthful. He could live according to what he considers truth, but he can't be Truth himself."

He'd never had a better friend than Timon, and Timon might be as smart as he was. He truly valued his friend's opinion. But even the smartest men could believe something that wasn't true.

"But even if something might be true, the value of truth has to be weighed against the cost of claiming it's true. I'm not willing to risk it. I lost my future in Cyrene. I'm not going to do anything to lose Caelus's good opinion of me and lose my future with him."

"I understand." Timon had been leaning forward. He drew back, but not like he'd been offended. His mouth relaxed into its usual smile. "Are you at least willing to learn more about why we believe in Jesus? To study it like a new philosophy to satisfy your intellectual curiosity about what Christians believe and why they're willing to die for it?"

Lusario crossed his arms. Timon so obviously hoped for a yes. It would do no harm to learn about a different philosophy, and it would make his friend happy. "I'm willing to do that, if only to un-derstand why it's illegal in Roman eyes."

"Good." Timon beamed at him. "I'll give some thought to how best to explain it, and we can talk later." He stood. "I'm so glad you've come back, and I couldn't be more pleased that you brought a good master with you." He tipped his head toward the library. "But he's probably waiting for you now, and Achilleus might be waiting for me. So, I'll see you later."

He slapped Lusario's upper arm and got a slap in return before each went to join the good men they served.

Inside the Great Library, Lusario strolled along the aisles of scrolls, looking for Caelus. He'd walked half the length of the main room when he heard the familiar voice.

"Thank you. I'll be talking with these to learn how I should proceed."

"If I can help further, don't hesitate to ask." The middle-aged man tipped his head to Caelus before walking away.

Caelus handed Lusario a papyrus sheet. "These are some of the people who lecture on building design and the engineering ap-proach to construction. I'll be talking to each to see if they do more than lecture. I'd like to find one who will guide me, telling me what I should read, what lectures I should attend. Maybe an expert who takes on a small group of people to study with him."

"There are philosophers who do that here. I expect you'll find someone." Lusario rolled the papyrus and handed it back to Caelus.

Caelus tapped his palm with the roll. "I'll start that tomorrow.

Right now, I'm ready to find the town house. I'd like to see what it's like, then arrange for the delivery of our baggage."

He led Lusario back into the garden. "I'm eager to meet the other men who lodge there. Perhaps you can point out some who are scholars, not ones like Florus who only look on Alexandria as a place for a good time."

"There were several when I left. Whether they're still here…" Lusario shrugged. It was only two months, but so much could change in that time.

They continued up Canopic Street, passing between the mausoleum where Alexander the Great's body was entombed and the gymnasium where men of all ages exercised and played games.

How many times had he walked past them and then looked north at the theater and the Caesareum, where the rites of the imperial cult were performed? Today felt like coming home. But for the man next to him, everything was new.

Caelus pointed at the Caesareum. "Cleopatra started building that to honor Julius Caesar and then Marcus Antonius, but Augustus finished it as a monument for himself and the later emperors." He directed his finger next toward the theater. "Julius Caesar used that as a fortress against a siege by the Egyptian royal troops when he got pulled into the dispute between Cleopatra and her brother." He rubbed his jaw. "Now that I see it, I think I'll reread the final book of Lucan's poem about Caesar's war with Pompey and the Senate."

Lusario's mouth twitched as he stopped the grin. To be in the city he loved with a man who was as excited as he had been when he first came here—nothing could be better. Except maybe seeing Florus's face as he learned how satisfied Lusario was with the turn his life had taken and all because Florus had tried to make his life miserable.

The morning he left for Carthago, his friends among the valets and houseslaves bade him sad farewells. Widened eyes followed by welcoming smiles were sure to greet him when they learned he had returned with a master who was a serious scholar and with the expectation of studying alongside him for the next three years.

A few short blocks and they reached the Latinus town house. Lusario's knuckles struck the expected pattern of knocks of a resident, and the door swung open.

The jaw of the youth pulling it open dropped. "Lusario?"

He placed his hand on Fylax's shoulder and squeezed. "I'm back with my new master, Caelus Publilius Martinus. He has a chamber rented here. Is the steward in his office?"

"He's out, but they just got one of the larger rooms ready for whoever was supposed to come this week." Fylax grinned at him as if sharing a private joke. "It's off the left balcony."

Lusario stepped back and motioned Caelus to enter ahead of him.

Fylax closed and bolted the door, then led them to the stairs. He pointed to an open door midway down the balcony. "It used to be Florus's."

Lusario grinned back. "I can take Master Caelus up myself."

At the doorway, he waved Caelus in ahead of him. He'd hated this room and the man who'd stayed here. But it was one of the best in the town house, with a view of the harbor through the window and a view of a fountain through the door.

Caelus strolled to the window and looked both ways. "Good

view and large enough." He pointed at the desk. "We'll need to get another for you. Something that will fit in that corner."

"Is Florus back?"

Lusario startled at the voice just behind him. He turned to find one of the lodgers who had the room just past Diokles's old chamber.

"No. I serve Caelus Publilius Martinus now."

The man's chuckle wasn't what Lusario expected. "That's good news for more than you." The Roman stepped into the room where he could see Caelus. "Martinus, welcome to Alexandria. I'm Gaius Vibius Fundanus. Can I assume you're from Carthago like Florus?"

Caelus tipped his head in acknowledgement of the greeting. "You can, but that's possibly the only way that I'm like Florus. I've come to study and learn, not merely enjoy myself."

Fundanus's snort accompanied friendly eyes. "Then you're nothing like Florus. Several of us are serious scholars here, and I, for one, welcome the addition of another." He tipped his head toward the doorway. "A few of us are heading to the baths after the morning lectures. Join me, and I'll introduce you."

"My pleasure." Caelus turned to Lusario. "Take care of what we discussed; then you may do what you want until dinner."

"Yes, Master."

As Caelus and Fundanus strolled down the balcony, descended the stairs, and headed back through the peristyle below him, their voices drifted up to Lusario.

"Fortuna smiled when you got Lusario. He took care of everything his old Cyrenian master didn't want to deal with. Or didn't know how to. I would have gladly bought him myself if Florus hadn't. If you ever want to sell him—"

"I won't. He's proven his worth several times over already."

If he believed in the Roman gods, Lusario would say Fortuna had not merely smiled. She'd chosen to favor him far beyond what he ever thought possible. He went to the window, where he could see Caelus walking toward the baths with Fundanus and two others that he knew to be good men.

Fortuna had smiled upon both of them.

Chapter 12

Midafternoon

In the corner of the chamber that was almost twice as large as the one he'd shared with Diokles, Lusario pushed his chest of notes under the narrow bed that had once been Famulus's. The two large travel trunks stood along the wall at the foot of it, and Caelus's chest of scrolls and codices sat by the cabinet. Florus had complained that the cubicle walls in the top half got in the way, but they were perfect for organizing the small library Caelus brought from Carthago. When his master returned from the baths with his new friends, Lusario would help him transfer everything from chest to cabinet, sorting as they did.

He straightened and rubbed his hands together. It was time to go to the shops by the harbor. He'd buy a roll of papyrus, the knife for slicing off sheets, bottles of ink, and fresh wax tablets before they went to their first lecture tomorrow. He'd also get a satchel to carry everything they'd both need at the library and lectures. If he found a small, cheap desk for the corner Caelus had assigned him, he'd get that, too.

He'd almost reached the shops when he paused midstride. Just ahead of him, Timon, swinging a large basket by its handle, came out of a building that had no sign saying what it was.

"Timon."

His friend glanced over his shoulder, then turned toward Lusario with a smile. "I didn't expect to see you today."

Lusario caught up with him. "Why the big basket?"

"I'm going to the market to get dried fruits and vegetables."

He nudged Timon's shoulder. "What did you do to get put on kitchen duty?"

A chuckle was Timon's first answer. "Nothing. It's for sharing with the poor."

Lusario resumed walking, and Timon matched his stride. "Why are you the one doing that?"

"It's something God says we should do—care for the widows and orphans, share our bounty with those who are in need."

"I suppose many are in need, although we don't see them much in this part of the city. So how do you find them?"

Timon glanced at him. "We have a list, but today I'm only shopping."

"I suppose you're doing this because Achilleus said to." Lusario rubbed his jaw. "We both do many things that a normal valet never would. But mostly I like that."

"He gives me money for it, but we both do it because God said to."

Because a god said to? Lusario fought the smile. "I've seen myself that Achilleus is an honorable man...and a generous one. I'm sure he knows what Seneca said about giving. 'We seek to do honorable acts, solely because they are honorable; yet even though we need think of nothing else, we consider to whom we shall do them, and when, and how.'"

First Timon chuckled, then he waved his hand as if to erase Lusario's words. "It's not a question of honor. It's a matter of agape, like I explained before you left. Love is a decision that we act upon, whether deserved or not. I don't deserve the love God has for me, but He bestows it anyway."

Lusario raised one eyebrow. "You think your god loves you?

"I know He does."

The certainty in Timon's voice—how could he possibly believe such a thing?

"What evidence do you have for that?"

Timon's eyebrows dipped, then relaxed. With one finger, he tapped his own chest. "The fact that I'm still alive. I don't know who my parents were, but whoever my father was, he wasn't Egyptian. They never expose a baby. When I was born, he decided I wasn't worth keeping. One of our cook's helpers decided to go a different way to the market that day, and he drove off some dogs that were fighting over me."

He touched his thigh. "The scars on my thigh and calf—they're from where one dog had hold of my leg and was dragging me away before another bit the other leg and tried to take me. Minio took me home and gave me to the wet nurse who was just weaning Achilleus's sister. Trophima wrapped me up to hide that I was hurt; then she asked the steward if she could feed me and raise me to serve in the household. He gave permission, and I've been part of Achilleus's household ever since."

Lusario wrinkled his nose. "You've only described the kindness of two people and a steward who wanted to get a free slave for his master. That's not the affection of any god."

"But God's hand was in it all. Minio sensed he should take a route he'd never taken before. He came by at just the right time to rescue me. I should have died, but he took me home, even torn and bleeding like I was, because he's"—Timon's voice dropped to a near-whisper—"a Christian, and Trophima wanted to care for me because she is as well. They wanted to give a baby that no one but God thought worth anything a chance to live." He glanced around them to make sure no one would overhear. "When Achilleus's father returned from his own father's estate and learned what they'd done, he was pleased because he's one, too."

"You haven't described anything that couldn't be explained by coincidence and the way some women dote on any small child, especially one they feel sorry for."

"God guides the choices His people make, when we let Him. Minio told me it felt like God was guiding his steps that day when he found me. He wasn't sure I'd survive what the dogs had done, but he asked God to help me. No matter how bad I looked, he knew God has the power to heal, and sometimes He does."

In the two years Lusario had known Timon, his friend had never revealed how he got the scars or his slight limp. And one slave didn't ask another such questions. But even if Timon believed what he'd just said, that didn't make it true.

"Asking a god to heal—that happens often at the Egyptian temples. Most people think a god has something to do with what happens, even when they choose what to do themselves. The Romans say Fortuna smiles. The Greeks credit the Fates or Tyche or Agathos Daimon. The Egyptians call the one controlling our fates Shai or

Shait, and they can't even decide if it's a god or a goddess. With so many choices, no one knows which is right or whether all of them are wrong."

"All of them are wrong, because there's only one God who's real, and He's the one we worship. For more than a thousand years, He's revealed what He wants people to know about Him through His prophets."

"A thousand years?" Lusario barely managed not to roll his eyes. "It's not even a hundred years since the procurator Pontius Pilatus executed your Jesus of Nazareth during Tiberius's reign. Tacitus wrote that Nero claimed Christians started the Great Fire in Rome. He executed them as arsonists, but it was not so much for arson as for their hatred of the human race that he killed them."

Timon's smile had vanished, and Lusario wished he could unsay what he'd just said. No one he'd ever known was less likely to hate anyone than Timon, and quoting what Tacitus wrote had hurt his friend.

Lusario shrugged and offered an ironic smile. "But maybe he was only reporting the official version of what happened. If Tacitus had known you, he couldn't have condemned all Christians as people filled with hatred."

"Histories are written by men aligned with the victors. Tacitus didn't know the truth of what happened under Nero or Pontius Pilatus." A hint of Timon's usual smile returned. "As a scholar, are you curious enough to hear the other side of the story and weigh both to decide where the truth lies?"

It wasn't something Lusario wanted to do. It could lead to disagreements that would ruin the best friendship he'd ever known. But in Timon's eyes lurked a laughing challenge that he couldn't easily refuse. Not without at least letting Timon present his version of the story.

"A man of honor should always want to know the truth. So, I'm willing to listen." He rubbed his mouth with the back of his hand. "But not today. I have to finish some errands for Caelus, and you need to get your vegetables. I'll be in Alexandria for the next three years, so we'll have many chances to talk."

"We will." Timon's smile expanded into a grin as he slapped Lusario's upper arm. "Until later."

As Timon walked away, he began humming one of the tunes Lusario had often heard when something had especially pleased his friend. He squeezed the back of his neck. The grin and that tune—why was Timon so certain he'd like those coming conversations?

The next morning

Caelus held his arms out, and Lusario wrapped the toga around him, adjusting the fabric to hang as well as he could. Most of the Romans wore their togas to the lectures, but only a few seemed to care about the elegance of the folds.

"I look the part of a scholar, but approaching Zenon to ask about studying with him…even the thought makes me nervous."

Lusario slung the satchel of tablets onto his shoulder. "The librarian thought he might consider it, so it's worth asking. After any lecture, some of those who listened gather around the speaker to discuss what he said. If you wait until the end of that, he should be willing to talk with you."

Caelus led them into the street and headed toward the library complex. At the entrance to Zenon's lecture hall, Lusario paused. "Wait a moment, Master."

They stepped to the side and let others enter ahead of them. "What?"

"I'll be sitting in the back row. At the front, the established scholars sit in the first two rows. Students and free people who simply want to hear that speaker use the third row and farther back." Lusario opened the satchel and withdrew two tablets and a stylus. "If you can sit on the aisle, I could bring down another if you need it."

"Good thinking." Caelus squared his shoulders. "Let's go learn."

Lusario slipped into the end chair in the back row and took out his own tablet and stylus. He blew out a long, slow breath. It was only the first lecture of many, and three years of learning lay ahead of him. But at the end waited a better future than he'd ever imagined.

The master of the hall raised his hand for silence, and those still standing sat. "Today we begin a series of lectures by a man renowned among the architects of Egypt and beyond." Palm up, he held his hand out toward a slightly stooped man with a fringe of silver hair and a well-groomed beard.

Zenon placed his fists on his hips and surveyed the room. "As today is the first of many lectures on architecture, I know some of you are here for the overview with which I always begin. Welcome. For those of you who aspire to become architects yourself, you are doubly welcome."

He strode to the podium. "Over the next few months, I shall discuss the work of many architects of renown. Some you may not have heard of before. Some you should know at least somewhat already, like Senenmut and Amenhotep, son of Hapu, who designed and built some of the finest temples at Thebes between 1400 and 1500 years ago. Another is Alexandria's own Hero, whose contributions are famous throughout the empire. Copies of his lecture notes on mathematics, mechanics, physics, and pneumatics can all be found in the Great Library. Consult them."

He rubbed his palms together before crossing his arms. "I shall show you design and engineering details of many of the best structures built for Emperor Trajan by Apollodorus of Damascus: the forum, the market, the baths, the bridges across the Danube during the Dacian Wars, the temple and column of Trajan in Rome. You will also study some of his technical treatises." A wry smile tugged at one corner of his mouth. "Strive to match his technical brilliance. But always remember the man who might hire you deserves proper respect, whether a wealthy freedman who knows nothing about good design or an emperor who draws up architectural plans himself."

Why such an admonition? Lusario rubbed his jaw. Hadrian had passed through Alexandria last fall, and his visit to the Great Library caused much excitement among the resident scholars. Had one of them forgotten what every slave knew: always show your master respect, even if he treats you like a friend?

"But principally you will be studying the writings of Vitruvius, whose *De Architectura* must be mastered by any who desire a career as an architect and engineer. There is no better presentation of the history and practice of engineering than his work. As you are able, I urge you to acquire your own copies of the ten volumes of this work. You will find it useful throughout your career."

Zenon rested his crossed arms on the podium and leaned toward his audience. "You will soon be designing buildings yourself, and when you do, follow Vitruvius's advice. 'All buildings must be executed in such a way as to take account of durability, utility, and beauty.'" He straightened and gripped both sides of the podium. "Now, we begin with an overview of the architects I consider most important."

Lusario glanced at Caelus and found his master leaning forward, as if the words Zenon spoke embodied great wisdom. Lusario gripped his own stylus, ready to record what he'd want to remember.

Three years in Alexandria learning from teachers like Zenon. Lusario couldn't stop the grin. The Romans would say Fortuna had smiled upon him. Timon would say prayers to his god had helped him get here. But whether some god was involved or it was merely happy coincidence, a life of challenges and opportunities like he'd always wanted lay ahead.

Chapter 13

Questions

Early afternoon

A constant murmur of voices surrounded Lusario as he and Caelus finished their lunch of bread and stew. A dining hall sat at the end of the garden between the library and lecture halls, and Caelus had chosen the outside seating for their first lunch after a lecture.

Caelus laced his fingers atop his head and arched his back. "For the first lecture here, I couldn't have chosen better. The librarian said Zenon was one of the best people for me to talk with to get started, and he was right. It's good you told me to sit on the end. I needed that third tablet. But I still didn't get everything down."

He picked up the cup of watered wine and swirled it. "Each day, I think we should compare notes and decide what's important to keep. Then you can make a copy of that on papyrus and set up a way to keep the sheets sorted so we can find any topic later."

With a quick backward tip of his head, Caelus drained the cup. "Father would laugh if he knew he'd sent me here with a secretary and more for the price of a house slave, all because Florus lied to his father about what you could do." He set the cup down. "I'll probably tell him in my next letter."

Secretary. That brought a smile to Lusario's lips. A respected position, second only to steward in the households of important men. "I can do that."

"Martinus."

Caelus raised his hand as Fundanus, also wrapped in his toga, approached.

Fundanus glanced at Lusario before focusing on his master. "I'm finished with lectures today, so I'm heading to the gymnasium and then to the baths. If you care to come along, I'll introduce you to some other scholars like ourselves."

Caelus slid his chair back and stood. "I'll take you up on that offer." His gaze shifted to Lusario. "You can do what you want this afternoon. You can start what we discussed after dinner."

"Yes, Master. I'll be at the library for a while before going home."

Caelus nodded once before turning and strolling away at Fundanus's side.

With satchel slung from his shoulder, Lusario headed to the library to read some of the first writings Zenon recommended. A good morning was turning into an even better afternoon.

As he walked through the reading room, a waving hand caught his eye. Timon sat at a table with a scroll open in front of him. With a curl of his fingers, his friend called him over.

"I was hoping to see you at the back of the lecture hall this morning. It was about establishing the trade routes to India." Timon spoke softly enough that no one at nearby tables would be disturbed.

"I went with Master Caelus to his first lecture. While we were talking yesterday, he got the names of some whom the librarian thought were the best lecturers on architecture and engineering. Zenon of Alexandria was at the top of the list. He studied with Tryon, who learned from Hero of Alexandria. Caelus already knew Hero was famous as one of the greatest engineers, so Zenon should be expert in what we want to learn."

"Were you impressed?" Timon leaned back in his chair.

"Oh, yes. He gave an overview of the most important engineers and what they did that made them important. It was the first of a series of lectures that should cover most of what we need to learn. Caelus spoke with him afterwards, and he recommended some writings in the library here that we should read as we begin our studies. I thought I'd look at the first of them while I'm free this afternoon."

He scanned the scroll panel that Timon had open before him. "What are you reading?"

"The Septuagint. It's a collection of writings with the oldest from more than a thousand years ago and the latest from five hundred years ago. It's history, poetry, prophesy, and so much more." Timon's slow smile accompanied bounced eyebrows. "It's God's own words to His people."

Lusario drew his head back. "Which god's own words? Egypt alone has over two thousand of them. Then there's the Greek and Roman pantheon and what the Germans worship and the Britons and the Parthians and…" He ended with a shrug.

Timon chuckled. "I know you're only teasing me. I already told you there's only one real God, and we follow Him."

With a slight tip of his head, Lusario looked down his nose at the scroll. "But it can't be something about your Jesus. You said the most recent writings there are five hundred years old. It's only a hundred years since Rome executed him."

"God has always existed. Jesus of Nazareth is how God came to earth as a man with a human mother but no human father. The Spirit of God is His father, so Jesus is both a man and God. These scrolls are God's words from before that time."

"Human mother and a god as the father?" Lusario wrinkled his nose. "This sounds like one of the stories about the gods of Olympus, where they get a human woman with child and their offspring are demigods."

"It's totally different. Let me explain." With a sweep of his hand, palm up, Timon invited him to sit in the chair across the table. Lusario hung the satchel from the back and sat.

Timon leaned forward, resting crossed arms on the tabletop. "Those are just ancient stories, not real events set in historical time." He glanced around them and lowered his voice. "Jesus was born during the reign of Augustus while Herod was a client king. He tried to kill Jesus when some magi came and asked where the newly born king was. Jesus's mother came from Nazareth, but Jesus was born in Bethlehem, as foretold by one of the other prophets four hundred years earlier. That's a few miles outside of Jerusalem."

Timon checked the nearby tables again to see if anyone was listening. "Just before Jesus was born, Mary's husband took her there for one of Augustus's censuses because he came from a family that lived there. But he didn't lie with her until after Jesus was born, so he wasn't Jesus's father. They came down to Egypt and stayed until after Herod died. Then they went back to Nazareth."

Jerusalem? Herod? Lusario pinched his lower lip.

Tacitus had written that was the capital of the Jews when Pompey took over Judaea. He'd gone into their temple, and they had no statues of their god. He went into their secret shrine, and it was totally empty. Marcus Antonius had made Herod a client king over Judaea, and Augustus left him in power. Was Timon saying he worshiped the god of the Jews?

Lusario's eyebrows plunged. "Did you say Jerusalem and Herod?"

As Timon drew back, his smile vanished.

"So the god you're talking about is the god of the Jews?" Lusario spoke the last word as if he'd like to spit it on the dirt and grind it with his heel.

"Yes and no." Timon raised both hands, as if to calm Lusario's anger. "He's the God over every land and all people. He created everything we can see and all that we can't. But He chose Abraham from Ur in the land of the Chaldeans to be the father of the people through whom He chose to reveal Himself. Abraham's grandson Jacob is the one whose descendants became the Jews."

Timon fingered the knob on one scroll rod. "This is the book of Isaiah. It's part of the Greek translation of the Hebrew scriptures. Ptolemy II asked the high priest in Jerusalem to send him Hebrew scholars who could translate so he'd have a Greek copy here in the library. It includes the story of God's dealings with His chosen people and the words He spoke through His prophets. About eight hundred years ago, Isaiah wrote down the prophesy God gave him about Jesus coming and what He would do."

He tapped the scroll knob. "That's what I was reading. It tells how God sent the suffering servant to—"

Lusario snorted. "I don't want to hear something from that scroll. Why would I want to know anything about the god of the people who destroyed Cyrene? I was thirteen when that murdering rampage started, and I'm only here now because Master Philandros heard they were coming. He fled with his family to Apollonia and escaped on a ship before they got to us. My father was tutoring his oldest boys then, so he took Father and me with him."

His teeth clenched. "Not all our people got away in time. When we returned, they had destroyed all the public buildings and torn up the roads. They killed most of the workers on the family estate east of town. Hadrian had to rebuild what they destroyed and bring in colonists just to work the land. I'm glad Trajan sent Turbo with a legion to get rid of every one of those murderers."

Timon rested his hand on Lusario's upper arm. "What they did was horrible. There's no excuse for it. They brought the war here, too, and when Lukuas's army defeated the Greek defenders some distance from town, the men who survived came to Alexandria and murdered every Jew they could find in the city. Not just the men who wanted to join in the battles, but women, children, and the men who wanted nothing more than to live in peace. A mother and daughter who joined us every week for worship were Jewish. Hannah was my age."

His gaze shifted from Lusario to something across the room. "One of our Roman brothers went in toga with his bodyguard to get them out before the mobs reached them, but they'd been cut down and left in the street before he could get there." When he focused once more on Lusario, old grief dimmed his eyes. "So, murder went both ways. But that all came from the evil choices of men who didn't know or didn't care what God wanted them to do."

"Hmph." Lusario's jaw had clenched, and he flexed it before he spoke. "What their god wanted them to do? Their leaders told them what they were doing was what their god wanted."

"But they should have known that wasn't true because what they did goes against God's most important commandments. God commanded his people not to murder. One could argue whether or not killing another soldier in battle is murder, but killing women, children, and the men who weren't soldiers, killing them all simply because the rebels wanted to get rid of anyone Greek or Roman—that's murder."

"It is, and they did it in the name of their god. Doesn't that make him just as responsible?" Lusario raised one eyebrow. The answer to his question was obvious.

"If I told you not to do something and you went ahead and did it anyway, should anyone blame me for what you did?"

Lusario's lips tightened. How did Timon always come up with a question that made the obvious seem like only one possibility?

"No…maybe. If you had the power to stop me and you didn't, then perhaps someone could. If the Jewish god is real, why didn't he stop the murdering?"

Timon might be good at that ploy, but he was at least as good.

With his middle finger, Timon rubbed his lower lip. "I don't know. But there are many things I don't understand at the moment that might become clear someday." He shrugged. "I'm only a man, so I see in part, but not the whole like God does."

One corner of his mouth lifted. "Like I told you at the quay, when I was praying for you the night before, I sensed God had something better for you than you expected. But I didn't know that meant you coming back here so I could talk with my best friend again."

He leaned forward and tapped Lusario's arm. "Maybe it was so we'd talk about this…and there's still much more I'd like to discuss."

Lusario leaned back and crossed his arms. "I said I'd let you tell me about your religion, like I'd listen to a lecture on some new philosophy. But it's curiosity only. I plan to remain a Stoic like Caelus and his family. Don't think you'll be changing my mind."

Timon's mouth twitched, like it did just before he made an unexpected winning move at the gameboard. "I don't expect to, but with God, you never know what will happen."

Across the reading room, Achilleus stood and raised his hand. With a curl of his fingers, he summoned Timon.

"Looks like your master wants you." Lusario rose and hung the satchel from his shoulder. "But it's time for me to read some from Vitruvius anyway, so I'll see you later."

Timon rolled the scroll and stood. With it cradled on one arm, he pointed toward the desk of the librarian. "Androkles will put this away for me and get whatever you need." He nudged Lusario's shoulder. "It's good to have you back."

"It's good to be back."

As they strolled across the room, Lusario glanced at his friend. With a master like Caelus and a friend like Timon, there was no place in the empire he'd rather be.

Chapter 14

The next morning

Since it was only two days until Zenon would present his next lecture, Lusario joined Caelus in the Great Library to read some of what the architect recommended. They were not the first to arrive, and the four copies of the first scroll of Vitruvius were being read by others. When one reader carried a scroll back to the librarian, Caelus walked behind him to get it next.

With the first scroll of Vitruvius open between them, Lusario finished reading each panel only moments before Caelus. They'd read the first thirty panels when Caelus laced his fingers atop his head and arched his back.

"When Zenon told us to read this first chapter on the education of the architect…" A deep sigh escaped. "Physics, geometry, and mathematics I expected, but I never dreamed it would include expertise in history, philosophy, and music and at least familiarity with medicine, law, and astronomy. Plus I need to know how to draw well and work with my hands."

He tapped Lusario's upper arm with his knuckles. "Looks like we have our work cut out for us if we're going to master what we need in only three years."

Lusario still held the knob on his end of the scroll to keep it open. "I like a challenge. From when I was here before, I already studied the main philosophers and some history. Also geometry and mathematics, but there might be more I need to learn."

Caelus rolled the scroll and stood. "I see why Zenon said every architect should have *De Architectura* in his own library. The later volumes provide such detailed information. I doubt we'll be laying out a city or building a temple, so we won't need all the scrolls, but I do want most of them."

"There are scroll vendors near here, but I don't know which would have it. I never bought anything from them."

"I'm meeting Fundanus for lunch at the town house. We're going to a few afternoon races at the hippodrome east of town. But on our way home, let's shop and see what we can find."

When they entered the first shop, a man sat at a desk at the back wall, facing the entryway while he copied a scroll onto a roll of papyrus.

He barely glanced at Lusario, but he rose and offered Caelus a friendly smile. "What may I help you with today?"

"I'm looking for a copy of Vitruvius, of *De Architectura*, to be specific."

"That can be very difficult to find, but you have come to the right place. I only just bought a copy from a scholar who was called home to deal with a family problem and needed enough for his ship's passage." He opened a cabinet with cubicles containing several dozen scrolls. From the top right, he removed one and placed it on the counter. "Used, but in good condition and ready to give years of service to its new owner."

Caelus opened the scroll. "This is the second book of the ten. What are you asking for it?"

"These are rare, but I offer the best prices in Alexandria. For this one, one hundred drachmas."

"One hundred? That seems high." Caelus inspected every panel, and the merchant's smile dimmed as Caelus worked his way to the end. "There are a few places where it's been repaired. But it seems to be in adequate condition for a used scroll. So, I believe I'll buy it if you'll take ninety."

"It's worth at least one hundred and twenty. But…" The merchant frowned, then shrugged. "You seem new here, and I sometimes give a discount when it's the first of many purchases you'll make here in the future. So, ninety-eight."

"Ninety-seven, and I'll take it."

"That's barely more than I paid for it, but today I'm feeling generous. For your first-ever purchase, ninety-seven is enough." The merchant's smile returned. "For only two drachmas more, I have a fine bag for you to store it in. A small amount to protect such a valuable scroll when you're not using it."

"I'll think about that." Caelus stroked under his chin. "Do you have the other volumes?"

"Other volumes?" The merchant's mouth twitched. "Which ones?"

"The first and numbers three through ten. I would like Vitruvius's entire work."

The merchant's lips pursed, and he blew out a slow breath. "These are very rare. To easily find a whole set of ten…that is not something a man can count on." His calculating eyes did not match the friendly smile. "But I have the solution to your problem. I could get custom copies made of the remaining nine scrolls."

"How much?"

The look of a cat who'd cornered a mouse flashed across the merchant's face. But it was so fleeting…had Caelus seen it?

"I gave you an extraordinary bargain on the second scroll because it was dirty and worn in places. So, it was a fraction of what a new copy would sell for. Since the others would be new, copied onto the finest papyrus using the best script, which takes more time, and with drawings painstakingly copied by artists themselves, each would be about nine times the price of the scroll you just bought."

Lusario barely stopped himself before he sucked air between his teeth. Even one of them would cost more than Martinus paid for him.

Caelus merely rubbed his jaw. "I'll think about that and get back to you. But I will be checking often to see if you get in another scroll that I want."

"I look forward to serving you." The scroll seller's eyes didn't match his oily merchant's smile.

When the door to the shop closed behind them, Caelus's mouth drooped. "That's far beyond what I could justify to Father. Are there other scroll shops that might have some I could afford?"

"There are some, but Vitruvius is not Seneca, where many copies are sold. I don't know if they'll have any. But…" He raised a finger. "What if I could find someone to make a copy from the one in the library? What would be reasonable to pay?"

Caelus's face brightened. "No more than half again as much as what I paid for this one. Do you know someone who can do that?"

"I don't, but my friend Timon might. He's lived here all his life."

"Ask him. Zenon said we need this, and from what I've read of the first scroll, I think he's right." He tapped Lusario's arm. "We need someone who can copy the drawings, as well, but that could be a different person."

Lusario rested his hand on the satchel. "I'll take this home so it will be safe, then I'll see if I can find Timon."

"Safe?" Caelus mouth twitched. "You sound like Regillus's steward."

"Didn't you notice the man who watched you buy it? He followed us out of the shop and turned away too quickly when I stared at him. In Alexandria, a thief can easily sell a scroll for good money, no questions asked. He might have been hoping we'd separate to make me an easy target."

Caelus looked over his shoulder. "I didn't notice. I'm always with someone else, but you often aren't." He fingered his lower lip. "Maybe you should carry the dagger."

"I was safe enough for two years here." Lusario touched the blue edging around the neckline of his fine linen tunic. "But this is better than anything I ever wore. It might seem I'm worth robbing now, so..."

"Carry it. Even when we're together, it will make you look like my bodyguard. Maybe that's safer for both of us." He plucked at the toga that restricted his left arm. "This symbol of status almost makes me a one-armed man. I thought Regillus's steward too cautious when he worried about me going unescorted into the city. Perhaps I was being reckless without knowing it."

Lusario's head drew back. As a Cyrenian tutor and valet, he knew next to nothing about being a bodyguard. But he'd wear the dagger, and merely looking like a man ready for trouble should keep trouble at bay.

"As you wish."

He wasn't tall, muscled, or able to scare even a child with his scowl. But he'd try his best to be a good bodyguard. Keeping Caelus safe as they pursued both their dreams meant more to him than his young master could ever know.

The Great Library, early afternoon

Lusario checked the reading room and found Timon with a scroll open before him. With steps as quiet as he could make them, he snuck up behind and looked over Timon's shoulder.

"God of Abraham, God of Isaac, God of Jacob? You're reading that supposed prophet again?"

Timon startled, then looked over his shoulder. "No. I'm reading the history of Moses demanding that the pharaoh free the people of Israel who'd been his slaves so they could return to Judea. That was the land that God promised Abraham would have for his descendants."

"Hmph." Lusario barely kept his eyes from rolling. "History? I never heard anything about any Moses who challenged a pharaoh and won. Nothing about a group of slaves being freed to return to their ancestral homeland."

Timon's grin was not what he expected. "If you were pharaoh, supposedly the earthly embodiment of Horus and a living god of Egypt, and the God of a group of slaves devastated your land until you let them go, would you inscribe that on your temple walls?"

Lusario's mouth twitched. Yet again, Timon had asked the question that only allowed the answer that supported his point.

He settled into the chair opposite Timon. "I didn't come to debate ancient history. I'm on an errand for Caelus. Do you know anyone who makes copies of scrolls?"

"Maybe. Why?"

"Would you find out whether they could make a copy of a scroll in the library? Eight scrolls, actually. Caelus would be willing to pay a reasonable amount for that."

Timon rested crossed arms on the desktop. "I can ask. He's always working on something, but he doesn't get paid."

"So, he's someone's slave?" Lusario rubbed behind his ear. A complication, but maybe Caelus could hire him through his master.

"No, but it's not how he makes a living."

"What is he copying that he works for free?"

Timon scanned the nearby tables. No one was sitting so close they might hear a whispered answer. "He makes copies of the gospel of Markos the Evangelist. Markos started the church where I worship. He was born in Cyrene, but his family moved to Jerusalem. He saw Jesus there. My friend also makes copies of the letters written by the apostles."

"Apostles?" The question slipped out before Lusario could stop it. He really didn't want to know.

"The men who knew Jesus when he was teaching in Judaea and Galilee. And Paul of Tarsus. He started out arresting Jewish followers of Jesus, but that changed after Jesus commissioned him to take the news of what He'd done on the cross to the people who weren't born Jews."

"Are you telling me your Jesus talked to someone after he was dead?" Before it started, Lusario stopped the eyeroll that claim deserved.

"After he'd been raised to life again, yes. He spoke to a few hundred people between his resurrection and when he returned to heaven forty days later. It was a few years after that he appeared to Paul when he was going to Damascus to arrest Christians. He commissioned Paul then."

"So, this Paul thought he had a vision. But those can be tricks of a man's mind."

"I wouldn't call it only a vision. He was knocked off his horse and blind for three days until God sent a believer to lay hands on him and pray. When his sight was restored, he knew he'd met Jesus. He spent the rest of his life obeying Jesus's command. Nero beheaded him in Rome for that. A year later here in Alexandria, Markos was teaching in a house church near the Serapeum. A mob seized him, tied a rope around his neck, and dragged him to death behind a horse."

Lusario blew out a breath through pursed lips. "Interesting stories, but you can tell me more some other time. Can you ask your friend? If he says yes, then we can talk about his fee and when he can do it."

"I usually see him when we meet on *Solis*, but he's out of town for a couple of weeks. I'll ask him next time I see him." He tapped the dagger hanging from Lusario's belt. "This is new."

"Caelus wants me to wear it. A thief started following us after we bought a scroll, and he thought it would make it safer when I was alone." He fingered the blue edge of his tunic. "Dressing too well for a slave puts me at risk like a free man. That was never a problem with Diokles or Florus." He tugged on the sleeve of Timon's quality linen tunic. "Achilleus puts you at risk, too, when you're alone."

Timon's chuckle was not what he expected. "But I'm never alone, and I have Someone protecting me that you don't."

Lusario crossed his arms. "Who would that be?"

"God." He'd dropped his voice to a near whisper.

Lusario pushed the word away with one hand. "If your god was any good at that, Paul and Markos would have died of old age, and his followers wouldn't have to watch who hears what they say." He kept his voice low, too. "Anyway, ask your friend when he returns. We'll also need someone who can copy the drawings. If he can do it, have him include that in what he thinks it will cost. If not, maybe he knows someone who can. Caelus can afford up to one hundred fifty drachmas per scroll."

"I'll ask that as well." Timon rolled the scroll and stood. "I have some errands to run. See you soon."

"Soon." As Timon carried the scroll back to the librarian, Lusario's hand settled on the handle of the dagger. Maybe he should find someone to teach him how to use it. But it was probably enough to wear it for show.

Timon might think his god protected him, but a man could keep himself mostly safe if he watched what was happening around him. He didn't need a make-believe god to take care of anything.

Chapter 15

Too Valuable to Lose

Near Cape Zephyrion east of Alexandria, two weeks later

Lusario leaned against the rail near the middle of the ship while Caelus sat under the passenger canopy with Fundanus. Although he couldn't hear their words, Caelus's hearty laugh at whatever Fundanus said sent a chill up his spine. Was history about to repeat itself?

For their first trip to view a nearby example of Greco-Egyptian architecture, Caelus had invited the man who was fast becoming his best friend in Alexandria. After the morning lectures, they'd begun spending most afternoons together. They went to the baths, then dined with friends of Fundanus who didn't live at the town house. The same had happened with Diokles. His old master had changed after Florus singled him out as the companion that he could turn into a devoted follower. Everything went downhill after that.

In the distance, he could see Cape Zephyrion and the Sanctuary of Arsinoe-Aphrodite. It had been built by Ptolemy II after he elevated his first wife, Arsinoe, to divine status, as he had been himself when he followed his father as pharaoh. With a dock right by the temple and its sacred grove, it gave Ptolemy's navy an easy place to stop and worship. He'd made his wife the patron goddess for his navy, and Aphrodite, with her supposed birth from seafoam, was believed to have special concern for sailors. But the sanctuary also drew unmarried women seeking her aide in getting a good husband.

As if any god or goddess cared what happened to anyone. One corner of Lusario's mouth lifted. Seneca had it right when he said religion that the common people believed to be true was known to be false by the wise. How the Egyptians could believe that becoming a pharaoh made a man a god or that such a man could make his wife a goddess was beyond understanding. Volero Martinus and Caelus were committed Stoics, like Seneca, and he would always be one himself.

A sudden splash drew his eyes from the distant temple to the water below him. A dolphin surfaced not twenty feet out from the ship, its fin slicing through the water before dipping below the waves again.

From the door of their room, he could see the dolphin fountain whose soft splashes were like background music as he combined the notes he and Caelus had taken each day. Whoever the sculptor was, he'd done a fine job of making it look like the animal that now swam near the ship as if it had found a friend.

It rose until its fin was out of the water, only to drop below the surface again. Then, for no obvious reason, it leapt out of the water as if it were flying through the air. After each leap, it stayed under for a long time before its fin broke through the surface once more.

Being so obviously fit for the water, why did it leap toward the sky?

Another joined it, and they set up a rhythm of first one, then the other, breaking the surface, almost like a dance. They moved next to the ship, and he leaned over the rail for a closer look.

He was straightening when—

"Demetrius!"

◆

Caelus lounged under the canopy with Fundanus. It felt good to leave the toga behind and wear only his tunic. But Lusario was right that wearing it in Alexandria brought respect without him doing anything in particular to earn it.

When someone shouted, "Man overboard," he glanced toward the sound. A sailor with an oar balanced on his shoulder stood where Lusario had been looking over the edge.

He strode to the rail where the man stared back along the ship's side. Lusario was in the water, face down. His body floated past the rudder.

None of the seamen had responded to the cry. They were leaving him behind.

Caelus ran toward the stern.

As he passed the canopy, he yelled at Fundanus. "Get the rowboat in the water!"

Arms extended with one hand atop the other, he dove into the sea.

When he surfaced, he scanned the waves. Fifty feet past him, Lusario floated, still face-down. Even with powerful hand-over-hand strokes, it seemed forever before he reached him.

He turned Lusario face-up and wrapped one arm around his chest from behind. With his free arm, he swam with sidestrokes toward the ship, keeping Lusario's face clear of the water. Someone was raising the sail to the yardarm, slowing the ship's passage through the waves.

They'd left his man to drown, but they wouldn't dare leave a Roman. At least not when another Roman would know they'd done it.

◆

Lusario's eyes opened to find blue sky above him and waves sloshing over him. Something pressed against his back, and he struggled to turn and grab whatever was keeping him above the water.

An arm tightened around his chest. "Stop fighting me." He'd know Caelus's voice anywhere. "Relax, and I will keep us both afloat until the rowboat reaches us."

It took all the willpower Lusario had to obey that command. But the arm held him securely as Caelus's other arm moved forward and back, pulling them through the water.

He heard a distant splash.

"The rowboat is coming." Caelus's grip on him never loosened, and his free arm kept moving. It seemed like hours, but the boat finally reached them. One of the seamen leaned over the edge to grab Lusario, and he pulled while Caelus pushed from behind.

He was on his hands and knees in the bottom of the boat, coughing up water, when the seaman helped Caelus into the boat as well.

Caelus squatted beside him. "Are you all right?" A hand rested on Lusario's back. "What happened?"

"I was leaning over the rail, watching a dolphin swimming beside the ship, and the next thing I knew, I was in the water with you holding me."

Caelus snorted a laugh. "You picked a poor time and place to swim with a dolphin."

They were almost back to the ship, which had tied up its sail to await their return.

Lusario twisted to sit so he could look into Caelus's eyes. How do you tell your master how much it meant that he jumped into the sea just to save you?

"Thank you for coming for me. You could have died doing it."

"Not likely. Father likes to race me in the pool at the Carthago baths. I swim almost as well as the dolphins." Caelus shrugged. "Besides, how could I go upriver where the locals only speak Egyptian if I don't have you along? And I couldn't afford a secretary who could catch anything I miss when Zenon gets excited and starts talking too fast." He slapped Lusario's arm. "You're too valuable to lose. So, be more careful. I can't start the business for Grandfather without my assistant."

They had reached the side of the ship, and a rope ladder was tossed over the edge.

"Can you climb up alone?" The smile had faded from Caelus's eyes, replaced by genuine concern.

"I think so." His head felt like it had when Florus slammed it into the wall as hard as he could.

"I'll be right behind you to make sure."

Lusario stood and gripped the side ropes of the ladder. He lifted one foot to the first rung, then the other. One rung at a time, leaving both feet on each rung for a moment as he tried to get his balance, he made his way up. When Lusario's head finally cleared the rail and he could see the deck again, Fundanus stood beside the captain, his mouth curved down. A sailor gripped both his wrists as he climbed the final two rungs and helped him get his legs over the rail. He took three steps before sitting on the deck. With three fingers, he felt a new bulge on the side of his head.

Caelus's head and chest appeared, and he gripped the rail as he stepped up on the gunwale. He swung his legs over and landed on both feet. As he squatted beside Lusario, he took Lusario's chin and turned his head to get a view of the bump.

"Whew. I expect you'll have a headache from that." He rested his hand on Lusario's shoulder. "I know you're as eager as I am to see the temple complex, but patience is a virtue. I've won more than one wreath in races at the *natatorium*, but even I know enough to wait for this ship to dock instead of swimming."

"I'm sorry, Master. The dolphins were right beside us. I was leaning over a little, but not so much I should have fallen." He touched the lump. "What hit me?"

"An oar. Good thing your head is as hard as mine." Caelus stood and held out his hand. "Come rest near the canopy until we reach Zephyrion. The ship will go on to deliver its cargo to Canopis and stop for us on its way back to Alexandria. We should have three or four hours to explore. You can walk with us if you're up to it or rest near the dock."

"I'll be able to walk with you."

No bump or headache would keep him from this chance to examine great architecture up close.

Caelus pulled him to his feet. "Good. Can you swim?"

"No. Cyrene is twenty miles inland, so no one saw the need."

Caelus kept their pace slow as they approached the canopy. Slow enough Lusario could pretend walking was no problem. With each step, that became more true.

"You're going to learn when we get back to Alexandria. We'll be taking the canals to different places, and I don't want to dive into one of those. I'll swim with dolphins, but not crocodiles." His crooked grin drew Lusario's grateful smile.

"Look." Caelus pointed toward the shore. "They aligned the temple to impress as we approach from the sea. The sanctuary is just beyond the docks, and the grove past the temple is designed for meditation. We'll want to note what plants and furnishings are used there. On a smaller scale, something like it might be a pleasing addition to a rural villa."

"Many would like that."

Fundanus had returned to a wicker chair under the canopy, but Caelus stayed at the rail beside Lusario as both gazed at the temple dedicated to a real woman and an imaginary goddess. Neither had the power to save a man who'd fallen into the sea.

But a man like Caelus did, and if he ever needed saving, Lusario would do everything in his power to rescue the master who'd risked dying to rescue him.

Chapter 16

A Matter of Loyalty

The library complex in Alexandria, two days later

As Lusario popped the last dried fig into his mouth, Caelus, who sat across the lunch table from him, tipped his head back to drain his cup. Then he raised his hand. Without even looking, Lusario knew Fundanus would be joining them. But the concerns he'd had about the growing friendship going the way of Diokles and Florus had ended at Zephyrion.

While he and Caelus had examined the temple and the gardens, making note of particular aspects they might use some day, Fundanus had joined their conversation, asking questions and listening to Lusario with almost as much interest as he showed Caelus. He would be a safe friend for his young master and maybe even for him as well.

"See you at home." Caelus stood. "There was a lot today. I'll want to go over your summary of what we both wrote down this evening. We're only going to stay for a few races, so I won't be late."

When Caelus joined his waiting friend, Fundanus even raised a hand to acknowledge Lusario before they strode away.

Some time in the library with another of Zenon's recommendations awaited him before he went home to combine their notes. But as he strolled past the lecture hall, Achilleus came out with Timon beside him. When Lusario waved, Timon spoke to Achilleus, who nodded. With his usual broad smile, Timon came to join him.

"I have good news. The man who copies scrolls is back in town. He's willing, but he needs to look at the scrolls you want copied before he can figure out what to charge. Someone is waiting for the copy of Markos he's working on right now, but he can start on the first of yours after that. You'll need to tell him which ones are more important to have quickly. He'll work them in with the free copy work he does as his service to God."

"I'll check with Caelus tonight and tell you which one tomorrow." Lusario massaged his neck. He didn't want to insult the man, but… "Before you talk to him again, can I see a copy that he's made to make sure Caelus will like the quality?"

"Maybe I can borrow one to show you." Timon scanned the people around them and spoke more softly. "We use some of his copies in our church."

Lusario lowered his voice to match his friend's. "I could go there with you now to see it. It won't take me long to decide."

Timon bit the corner of his lip. "I have to ask the fellowship if it's all right to let you do that. I trust you to know what I am, but that doesn't mean they will feel safe letting you see where we meet. Rome has made our faith illegal, so we don't hang out a sign proclaiming what happens behind our closed doors."

With his thumb, he rubbed his palm. "We have to be careful about strangers." His eyes spoke a silent question when he turned them back on Lusario. "But if you wanted to learn what Jesus did and were considering whether to join us in following him, that would be a different matter."

Lusario's snort was quiet enough not to draw anyone's attention. "I told you already that I'm willing to learn about what you believe as a philosophy, but I'm a Stoic. I'm not looking to find anything to worship."

"Then I'll have to get permission." Timon's wry smile was punctuated with a shrug. "But you and I can still enjoy discussing what I believe as a philosophy you don't yet understand." He tapped Lusario's arm. "You haven't told me about your trip yet. What was the most impressive part of it?"

"We were almost to Zephyrion when I got hit in the head and knocked into the sea."

Timon's head drew back. "You what?"

"I was leaning over, watching some dolphins right by the ship when someone accidentally hit my head with an oar, and I fell in. It knocked me out for a while, too."

"Thank God someone rescued you." Timon blew out a slow breath. "You came as close to dying as I did with the dogs before God brought Minio to save me."

"No god had any part in saving me. Caelus dove into the sea to do it. He risked dying to keep me from drowning. I owe him my absolute loyalty for saving my life, and I intend to pay that debt."

Timon's hand rested on his shoulder. "'Greater love has no one than this, than to lay down one's life for his friends.'"

"Exactly. You used *agape* there, the love that's a decision and the desire for what's best for the friend. That's what Caelus did. I don't expect close friendship from any master, so *agape* is a better word than *storge* for why he did it."

"Do you know who said that?"

Why did Timon have that smile that crept out when he'd just set down the winning game piece?

"I probably should." Lusario rubbed his jaw. "But I don't recall."

"Jesus. He said it to His disciples right after He commanded them to love each other like He had loved them. Then He did what He'd told them to do. To save them and me and anyone else who would ever believe in Him, He let Himself be sacrificed on a Roman cross to be the perfect blood sacrifice that would remove the barrier between us and God."

Lusario's jaw dropped. "Your religion is based on human sacrifice? You're the last man I would ever expect to approve of that."

No wonder Rome had declared this Christian religion illegal. The Romans put a stop to that wherever they found it. The old Carthaginians who fought three wars with Rome, the Druids in Germania and Britannia—human sacrifices to their gods ended when Rome defeated them.

"It's not like you're thinking. Not an ordinary person sacrificed to appease an angry god. God told Moses what people must do to approach him. For over a thousand years, the blood of animals that had no defects had been used, not to appease God's anger, but to temporarily cover the people's sins so they could be in His presence. The sacrifice of a valuable animal showed their repentance for what they'd done…or failed to do."

Timon scanned the area around them again. "Those sins built up a barrier separating them from fellowship with God. God is perfect, pure, and holy. He can't tolerate sin in His presence. But even though we don't deserve it, His *agape* love is so great that He came to earth Himself as a man, as Jesus. He chose to die as the perfect sacrifice, not just to cover sin but to finally tear down all the barriers between us and God. All we must do is believe."

His eyes had an uncomfortable intensity as he fixed them on Lusario. His usually laid-back friend leaned in, as if waiting for Lusario's response.

Lusario fingered his lip. Should he stop this discussion before it went further? If the wrong person came close enough to hear, Timon could be in danger. But something niggled at the back of his mind, warning that he'd regret that.

Curiosity overcame discomfort, and he couldn't stop himself from asking another question. "Those barriers you call sin—what exactly are they?"

Timon nodded toward their favorite bench. "Let's sit over there out of the way where no one can come up behind us."

Palm up, Lusario invited his friend to lead the way.

Timon sat on one end and turned toward him, but he kept glancing away to make certain no one came near enough to hear. "Remember what Tacitus wrote about how Judaea became subject to Rome? How Pompey entered the temple after he took Jerusalem. He found no statues of the Jewish god there and nothing at all in their secret shrine when he entered."

Lusario crossed his arms and nodded. Why would anyone build a temple, only to put nothing in it? But maybe the priests had just hidden everything before Pompey got there.

"There were no statues because God commanded his people to never make images to worship. Anything made by human hands could never be worthy of worship as if it were a god."

"That's true." From what Lusario had seen, some men deserved admiration, but nothing was worthy of worship. "But what does that have to do with what your god thinks you shouldn't do?"

"After Moses led the Israelites out of Egypt, God gave him the *Dekalogos*, the Ten Words, on Mount Sinai. They show us how God wants us to live. Moses wrote them down first and read them to the people. Then God inscribed them on two stones as a covenant between Him and Israel. Four are about us and God. Six are about how we should treat other people."

"Your god who supposedly defeated a pharaoh gave the man who led those people verbal instructions?" Lusario's eyes narrowed. Oracles claimed the gods spoke to them, but no one else ever heard them do it. Without a witness, the truth of any claim remained unproven.

"He did, and the people heard God speaking, although they didn't all understand what He said."

A group of men passed by thirty feet from them, and Timon leaned closer. "The first is the most important. We're to have no other god than Him. That's why we won't take part in the imperial cult, even if that means dying. The second tells us not to make and worship any idol, so Pompey found no statues. The third tells us to never take God's name in vain. No cursing with His name, no oaths using His name because our simple yes or no to another is as binding as an oath. And no mocking Him."

"But what was the point of an inner sanctuary if they didn't put anything in it?"

"There used to be something. The stone covenant tablets were there in a gold-plated ark, but the ark was taken away and hidden before the Babylonians took Jerusalem and destroyed the first temple six hundred years ago. What the priests did with it is a mystery.

The temple Pompey entered was the one they built when they returned from exile under the Persians."

A quick glance around revealed no one close enough to hear, and his friend relaxed. "The fourth says to remember and keep the sabbath holy. God set aside one day a week when we gather with other believers and worship Him."

Timon lowered his voice, even though no one stood nearby. "Rome is afraid when people assemble that they might be plotting some kind of rebellion, so they forbid our worship gatherings. The law treats them the same as a riot. This is why the elders are careful about who learns where we meet and when, but what God wants is more important than any decree of an emperor."

"Ignoring Roman law is a dangerous thing to do."

"Doing the right thing is more important than doing what's safe."

Lusario drew a deep breath and held it before blowing it out through pursed lips. In principle, Timon was right, but acting on that could get his friend killed. It was time to get this conversation finished before the wrong person heard any of it.

"That's four. You can tell me the others another time."

"I'll shorten them, but they're important to know."

Lusario suppressed a sigh. Timon never stopped until he'd made his points. "Make it quick. Too many people might hear after another lecture gets out."

"The others have to do with how we treat other people. Jesus summarized it quite simply. We're to love others like we love ourselves. If we do, we won't murder or steal or lie to get someone in trouble or begrudge the good things another person has, wishing we could make them our own."

"Sounds like good Stoic teaching." One corner of Lusario's mouth lifted. "If you hadn't said your Moses lived a thousand years ago, I'd say he'd been studying with Zeno or Seneca."

"But it's not just philosophy. What we believe about Jesus has eternal consequences. Caelus saved you from drowning this time, but the day will come when you will die. Who's going to save you then?"

Lusario's head drew back, and he gave Timon the frown that question deserved. "You know what Seneca said. 'There is nothing after death, and death itself is nothing.' Perhaps there's nothing to be saved from. Maybe we just cease to exist."

"Oh, no." As Timon's gaze bored into Lusario, he slowly shook his head. "That's not what happens. The essence of us, our soul, lives on past our body's death. After we die, we either spend eternity with God or go to a place of outer darkness. We make the choice ourselves by accepting the forgiveness of God that Jesus made possible or by rejecting it." His hand rested on Lusario's shoulder. "I want my best friend with me for eternity, not lost forever."

An odd feeling in the pit of Lusario's stomach made him clench his teeth.

"Well…" He rubbed his lower lip. "Maybe what you believe is true, maybe not. What you've said is…thought-provoking, but it's not enough to convince me to become a Christian. Whether your god saves people…" He drew a breath through his teeth. "Maybe he does; maybe he doesn't. But I do know two things. I owe my life to Volero Martinus for rescuing me from Florus before he got me killed and to Caelus, who risked his own life to save mine. My loyalty belongs to those two men, and I would never want to offend them by abandoning my Stoic beliefs for a god I'm not certain even exists."

Timon blew his next breath out through his nose. "I understand. But the true scholar is always open to discussing ideas with good friends. I hope we'll keep doing that."

Lusario chuckled. "What you mean is you haven't given up on convincing me. You can keep trying. You'll have at least three more years while we're studying in Alexandria. Just don't expect to succeed."

Timon's straight lips relaxed into the smile that greeted Lusario whenever they met. "Only time will tell. And no matter what you decide in the end, you'll still be the best friend I've ever had."

Timon shifted his gaze to a movement across the courtyard. Achilleus stood with a group of men, summoning Timon with his raised hand.

Timon rose. "See you soon."

"Looking forward to it."

As Timon hurried to join his master, Lusario's wry smile relaxed into a happy one. Any man with a friend who cared so much about his future and a master who had risked dying to save him was rich in what really mattered. Timon would say he was blessed; the Romans would say Fortuna had smiled on him. But even if none of their gods were real, the hopeless ending of his old life had become a hope-filled beginning. Could anyone ask for more?

Lusario and Caelus have only begun their studies,
and Timon hasn't given up.

So, stay tuned for what happens three years later
in the rest of their story, *River of Life*.
Join me again in Roman Egypt
when God reveals there is so much more.

I'd Love to Hear from You!

If you enjoyed this book, it would be a real gift to me if you would post a review at the retailer you purchased it from. A good review is like a jewel set in gold for an author. Other great places to share reviews are Goodreads and BookBub. If you've read others in the series, it would be great if you post a review of those, too.

I'd also love to hear from you at carol-ashby.com or directly at carolashbyauthor@gmail.com.

Want to hear about upcoming releases in the Light in the Empire series and free gifts only for newsletter subscribers?

For free gifts and other special offers, advance notices of upcoming releases, and info about my latest writing adventures, please sign up for my newsletter at https://carol-ashby.com/newsletter/.

Light *in the* Empire Series

Dangerous times, difficult friendships,
lives transformed by forgiveness and love.

Crushed Hopes and Hopeful Beginnings is the latest volume in the Light in the Empire series, which follows the interconnected lives of several Roman families during the reigns of Trajan and Hadrian. Each can be read stand-alone. The novels of the series will take you around the Empire, from Germania and Britannia to Thracia, Dacia, North Africa, Egypt, Judaea and, of course, to Rome itself.

Although each can be read stand-alone, here are some groupings based on the appearance of some characters in more than one story.

Drusus family: *The Legacy, True Freedom, Second Chances, Forgiven*

Lentulus family: *Blind Ambition, Faithful*

Crassus family: *Blind Ambition, Faithful, Honor Bound*

Sabinus family: *The Legacy, Honor Bound, More Than Honor, What Matters Most*

Glabrio family: *What Matters Most, Truth and Honor*

Titianus family: *True Freedom, More Than Honor, What Matters Most, Truth and Honor*

Brutus family: *Faithful, True Freedom, Honor Bound*

Martinus family: *Truth and Honor, Crushed Hopes and Hopeful Beginnings, River of Life*

The Dacians: *Hope Unchained, Hope's Reward, True Freedom*

More info on times, locations, and families in each book is at https://carolashby.com/novel-relationships/.

COMING IN 2024: PLEASE HELP ME CHOOSE!
Who would you like to see in a future story?

Since *Crushed Hopes* is the backstory of several of the men who will be major characters in *River of Life* (releasing in 2024), I already know which story I'll be writing next. But I'm always looking for the next hero or heroine, and fans of the books in the series often tell me who needs to come back as a story lead.

I delight in responding to those requests. People who loved Galen as a teen in *Blind Ambition* asked to see him as a grown man, so he returned in *Faithful.* That story is set eight years later when his faith in God and loyalty to a friend made a world of difference to three other people. Fans of Brutus and Africanus in *True Freedom* learned their fate in *Honor Bound,* and anyone who wondered where Ursus the gladiator in *Hope Unchained* went could find out in *Hope's Reward.*

Sometimes it's what happened earlier that people long to know. So many people asked what happened to Leander's long-lost sister in *True Freedom* that I couldn't resist giving Ariana her own story in *Hope Unchained.*

If you've already read *Truth and Honor* set in Carthago, you might have wondered about Volero's son, who was expected to return shortly from Alexandria in Egypt. You'll be able to find out soon in *River of Life,* the next full-length adventure in the Light in the Empire series that's set in Roman Egypt. I hope this backstory of how Caelus and Lusario got together and became friends has whetted your appetite for finding out what happens three years in the future and a year after Grandfather has died.

There are many more characters in the books of the series that I would like to spend more time with, and I hope there are some for you, too. Who would you most like to see in a future story? What was it about them that made you want more of them? I'd love to hear what you think. It will guide what I write after *River of Life*.

Some possibilities:

Aulus of *True Freedom?*

Septimus or Manius of *Honor Bound, More Than Honor,* and *What Matters Most?*

Someone else I haven't mentioned? (I can't wait to see who shows up here!)

Please tell me who you'd love to see again as a comment at carol-ashby.com or directly at carolashbyauthor@gmail.com!

Sign up for the newsletter at my website, and you'll be among the first to find out what's coming next. Looking forward to hearing from you!

Historical Note

ALEXANDRIA, THE GREATEST LIBRARY OF ANCIENT TIMES, AND THE SEPTUAGINT

Alexandria was founded on the shore of the Mediterranean by Alexander the Great in 331 BC. He built it to be his new capital of Egypt. It remained the capital for almost a thousand years until the Muslim conquest of Egypt in AD 641. It lay just east of the Egyptian town of Rhacotis, which would become the Egyptian Quarter of Alexander's city. Unlike most ancient cities that grew rather haphazardly over time, this new Greek city was designed by Alexander's favorite architect, Dinocrates of Rhodes.

On a narrow strip of land between Lake Mariotis and the sea, Dinocrates laid the city out in a grid. Two main streets, each 100 feet (30 m) wide, crossed near the city center, where Alexander's tomb would later be built. Side streets were 20 feet wide and paved with cobblestones. New canals connected the city with a then-major branch of the Nile (the Canopic or Canobic), which has since dried up. By diverting rivulets under the main streets, wealthy homes had fresh water delivered to them. A bridge connected the city with Pharos Island, which sheltered the harbor area. At 3900 feet (1200 m) long, it divided the old single harbor into an eastern military harbor and a western commercial one.

After Alexander's death in 323 BC, four of his generals divided the empire, and Ptolemy Soter took possession of Egypt. Also known as Ptolemy I, he started the Macedonian dynasty of pharaohs that would end with the suicide of the famous Cleopatra VII in 30 BC when Octavian (later Augustus) captured her in Alexandria and ended the civil war with Mark Anthony.

Both Ptolemy I Soter and his son, Ptolemy II Philadelphus, undertook major building programs, turning Alexandria into one of the premier cities of the ancient world. In the center of the city near Alexander's tomb, they erected many public buildings in the classical Greek style. These included the Mouseion (Museum in Latin), the Great Library, lecture halls, and the Great Theater.

They replaced the bridge that Dinocrates built with a broad causeway (mole), the Heptastadion, named for its seven-stadia (0.7 mile or 4100 feet) length. Two bridges let some smaller ships move between the eastern Great Harbor and the western Port of Eunostos. They built the lighthouse of Alexandria (the Pharos) at the eastern end of the island, marking the Great Harbor entrance. Started by Ptolemy I and finished by Ptolemy II, it took twelve years to build. At 453 feet (138 m) high and visible from almost 50 (80 km) miles at sea, it was one of the Seven Wonders of the Ancient World.

Ptolemy II restored a canal originally built by Rameses II to connect Lake Mariotis to the Canopic branch of the Nile, so the bountiful crops grown where the Nile flooded could reach the river port on the south side of Alexandria. After becoming a Roman province in 30 BC, Egypt was the personal property of the emperor. It supplied one third of the grain needed to feed Rome. Since the wheat from vast areas of Egypt could be brought to Alexandria on its many waterways, Alexandria was home to the imperial grain fleet that delivered that bounty to feed a hungry city. Under Augustus, Egypt provided around 150,000 tons (140 million kg) of wheat to Rome each year.

Ptolemy I Soter wanted to make Alexandria into a center for scholars, much as Athens had been for centuries. To attract top scholars from the intellectual centers in Alexander's old empire, he built the Mouseion (Museum in Latin), which was a shrine to the Muses, the nine Greek goddesses of literature, science, and the arts. As part of it, he began a library collection that he hoped would become the greatest in the Greek-speaking world.

His son, Ptolemy II Philadelphus, shared the same vision. He expanded the Mouseion, adding additional library space that became known as the Great Library, lecture halls, and gardens. He hired resident scholars, giving them free room and board and a salary for studying and teaching there. Among the intellectual greats who studied there were Eratosthenes of Cyrene who calculated the circumference of the earth, Aristarchus of Samos who proposed a sun-centered solar system, Euclid who is called the father of geometry, and the famous mathematician and inventor Archimedes.

Philadelphus's son, Ptolemy III Euergetes, built the Serapeum in the western part of the city. It was a sanctuary for the cult worship of the Greco-Egyptian god Serapis. The cult of Serapis was created by Ptolemy I and promoted by later Ptolemies to merge Greek and Egyptian religious traditions. Serapis already existed as an Egyptian deity, combining the Egyptian gods Apis and Osiris, but the cult added some characteristics of the Greek gods Hades, Demeter, and Dyonisus. Serapis was the patron god of the Ptolemies and later became popular in many parts of the Roman Empire.

As part of the Serapeum complex, a branch of the Great Library was built to house part of the massive collection of scrolls accumulated by the early Ptolemies. The Ptolemies used several methods for adding material to the library collections. Some were simply purchased, but any ship that landed in an Egyptian port was searched for scrolls. Any writings that were not already in the library were seized and copied. The original scroll was sent to the Great Library while the copy was returned to the original owner.

To make the great works of many cultures available to Greek-speaking scholars, both residents and visitors, Ptolemy II provided large sums of money to his chief librarian to buy "all the books in the world" for his library. He also paid to have Greek translations made of many works originally written in other languages. The greatest contribution Ptolemy II Philadelphus made to civilization came from that policy, and the spiritual impact of that decision is still being felt today.

The Septuagint, the standard Greek translation of the Hebrew Scriptures and the one used by Jesus and his apostles, was prepared in Alexandria around 250 BC. How that happened is told in a letter from Aristeas, a government official and scholar who was involved in the process, and in the writings of Philo of Alexandria in AD 15. The letter of Aristeas to his brother was reproduced in Josephus's *Antiquities of the Jews* around AD 93.

As the wisdom and historical literature of many cultures was being gathered and translated, the head librarian for the Great Library, Demetrius Phalereus told Ptolemy II that they should include the writings of the ancient Jewish culture and that skilled translators would be needed. Ptolemy told him that he had already given him the money for that, so do it.

Ptolemy had a letter sent to High Priest Eleazar in Jerusalem. He asked Eleazar to send translators, "choosing men of honorable lives, advanced in years, who are skilled in the Law and able to interpret it, out of each tribe six, so that agreement may be obtained from the large number, because the inquiry concerns matters of great importance."

Aristeas and Andreas, one of Ptolemy's chief bodyguards, traveled to Jerusalem with twenty cups of gold, thirty of silver, five bowls, a table for offerings, and a hundred talents of silver for offering sacrifices and for whatever repairs the temple might need in the future.

In response, the high priest sent six scholars from each of the twelve tribes to perform the translation. Philo of Alexandria, writing in AD 15, describes the activities of the translators in *The Laws of Moses Vol. II*. At a dinner with Ptolemy when they arrived in Alexandria, the pharaoh posed many questions to them. He was impressed with the intellectual excellence of the translators and told them to start their work.

They selected a secluded location on the Island of Pharos to do their translation. Philo reports that there was total agreement in the selection of each word of the translation, even when alternative Greek words might be used for a Hebrew word. He ascribes this to the men being not merely translators, but prophets directly inspired by God as they worked. Before and during Philo's time, there was an annual celebration by Jews and others on the island to give thanks for God's word being translated into Koine Greek, which made it accessible throughout the Hellenized world.

The importance of inspired word selection is seen in the translation of the Hebrew word *almah*, which refers to a young woman of childbearing age. For all but two occurrences of *almah*, the Septuagint translates it using *neanis* (νεᾶνις), meaning young woman or maiden. But for those two exceptions found in Genesis 24:43 and Isaiah 7:14, *almah* is translated as *parthenos* (παρθένος), the word meaning virgin in Greek. The Isaiah prophesy of a virgin conceiving and giving birth to a son foretold how Jesus would enter this world.

The translation, paid for by a Greek pharaoh as just one of many ancient literary and cultural documents, was quickly recognized as the authoritative version of the Jewish holy book by the Jews who didn't use Hebrew in daily life. For those who had settled throughout vast areas of Europe, Africa, and Asia, Koine Greek was their common language. Since many of these diaspora Jews were no longer fluent in Hebrew, the Septuagint was regarded as the official words of God, equal in authority to the original Hebrew writings.

When the apostles, including Paul, quoted Old Testament scriptures, it was usually the Septuagint translation that they used. When Paul took the Gospel into the Gentile world, the scriptures that were read in the Jewish synagogues would often have been from the Septuagint since Koine Greek was the language the local Jews and Gentile God-fearers would all know. Many if not most would have had difficulty understanding Hebrew. Similarly, all the books of the New Testament were written in Koine Greek, making them easy to understand in most of the eastern Roman Empire.

The Great Library has been gone since the 7th century AD, and the history of its destruction has some interesting twists. When Julius Caesar brought troops into Alexandria to help settle the dispute between Cleopatra VII and her brother, a building that housed part of the library in the Royal Quarter was accidentally set afire.

After Augustus (Octavian) defeated Mark Antony and Cleopatra VII, Egypt was reduced from powerful kingdom to Roman province. The library no longer had the patronage of a pharaoh. It became less important as other libraries around the Roman Empire grew. Claudius built an addition, but he appears to have been the only imperial patron. Other libraries opened in Alexandria, including one in the temple where the emperors were worshiped, and some of the Great Library holdings might have been used to stock them.

The Imperial Library in Constantinople, started by Constantius II, the son of Constantine, became the greatest repository of Greek and Latin literature, housing more than 100,000 texts until at least the 1200s.

Some accuse Christians of being responsible for the destruction of the Great Library collection during the reign of Emperor Theodosius, when the Serapeum, the cult sanctuary of Serapis, was destroyed in AD 391. But destruction of the pagan temple doesn't require the destruction of the library holdings. There is solid historical evidence that this wasn't the end of the library.

What remained of the Great Library was destroyed in AD 642, when Christian Alexandria was overrun by the Muslim army under Amr ibn al-As. A Muslim historian, Abd al-Latif, reported in the late 1100s that the general contacted Caliph Omar to ask what to do with the still-massive collection. According to Abd al-Latif, Omar replied, "If those books are in agreement with the Quran, we have no need of them; and if these are opposed to the Quran, destroy them." His general proceeded to burn the entire collection. The scrolls from the great library were reputedly used to heat the baths in Alexandria, and there were enough to heat it for 6 months. If you're interested in reading the works of Josephus or Philo in the original Greek or in English translation, I recommend the Delphi Ancient Classics series of e-books, available for very low prices at

Amazon. For this historical note, I consulted the works of Josephus and Philo.

For the novella, *Crushed Hopes and Hopeful Beginnings*, I also used the Delphi Ancient Classics editions of Tacitus, Seneca, Strabo, Polybius, Herodotus, and Pliny the Elder.

Interested in more articles about many aspects of life in Roman times? Check out my website, Life in the Roman Empire: Historical Fact and Fiction at carolashby.com.

Discussion Guide

1) Lusario was born a slave in a Cyrenian household where his father, also a slave, was a tutor first to the family sons and then for pay. Lusario expects to do the same and to be allowed to keep some of the money he earns for his master so he can buy his freedom. Then the foolish action of another person crushed any hope of that. How did Lusario respond? Have you or someone you know ever been faced with the actions of someone else making your dreams or goals impossible? How does our faith in God affect our response?

2) Sent by his father to finish his education, Diokles came to Carthago as a decent young man. What changed after he met Florus? Diokles's father expected Lusario to keep Diokles out of danger in Alexandria. The father assumed his son would listen to Lusario's good advice, but Diokles listened to Florus instead. Lusario starts with influence but no authority, then he loses any influence. Have you or anyone you know been faced with this dilemma? Was there a good solution?

3) Florus picked Diokles as his closest friend. Why do you think Florus chose him? How would you describe their relationship? Have you ever watched someone you cared about be led astray by someone they considered a good friend? Did anyone try to stop it and succeed? What worked or didn't work?

4) As the only son in a wealthy political family, Caelus Martinus was expected to follow in the footsteps of his father and grandfather.

But he wanted something different. What does that tell us about him? How did his relationship with his Christian cousin affect him?

5) As a baby, Timon was rescued from certain death by some Christians, then grew up to be a Christian himself. How did that affect his approach to life's problems?

6) Why did Achilleus try to help his valet's friend? What came of his attempt? How did Lusario respond when he learned what Achilleus had done and why he'd done it?

7) Timon and Lusario has been friends for many months before Timon revealed he was a Christian. Why did he wait? How did he first share what he was? How did Lusario respond? Have you ever had the chance to talk with a non-believing friend about your faith? How did you decide it was the right time? How did they respond?

Glossary

Agape: unconditional love, an act of the will, not an emotion

Agora: market area

Brucheum: Greek quarter of Alexandria, east of the library and lecture halls

Caldarium: A hot, steamy room at a Roman bath complex with tubs of hot water sunk into the floor

Chiton: a simple tunic of light linen, usually pleated, worn with a belt

Corbita: a large merchant ship

Drachma: the Roman Egyptian coin worth one denarius

Duumvirs: two men who served together as mayors of a city

Epicurian: follower of a philosophy that considered happiness and avoiding pain or emotional upset as the greatest good. The pursuit of pleasure was prized by Epicurians.

Eros: romantic love

Himation: rectangular cloak that passed under the left arm to be secured at the right shoulder

Hippodrome: racetrack for chariots, also called a circus

Latrunculi: military strategy board game involving trapping and removing captured stones

Natatorium: a swimming pool

Paterfamilias: the oldest living male of an extended Roman family, the patriarch who owns everything

Phileo: love between friends

Res mortales: mortal thing, the legal term for a Roman slave

Salve: hello, the standard Roman greeting

Serapis: Greco-Egyptian god who combined the Egyptian gods Osiris and Apis with the characteristics of the Greek gods Hades, Demeter, and Dyonisius. The Cult of Serapis was promoted by Ptolemaic pharaohs to unify Greek and Egyptian temple worship.

Solis: Sunday

Stoic: follower of a philosophy that uses self-control and fortitude to overcome excessive emotions. They value reason based on logic and the rules of nature. Zeno, Seneca, and Marcus Aurelius are famous Stoics.

Storge: love between family members

Strigil: a metal scraper used to remove oil, sweat, and dirt

Tabula: popular Roman board game, often played with betting, similar to backgammon

References from Scripture and Ancient Literature

CHAPTER 4

The greatest commandments: Mathew 22:37-40, Mark 12:28–34, Luke 10:25–28

CHAPTER 11

Jesus as the Way, the Truth, and the Life: John 14:6

CHAPTER 12

Sharing with those in need: Matthew 25: 41-45

Procurator Pontius Pilatus: Luke 3:1, Matthew 27, Mark 15, Luke 23, John 18.

CHAPTER 13

Jesus's human mother and God as his father: Luke 1:31-35

Jesus's birth during the reign of Augustus while Herod was a client king: Luke 2:1-5, Matthew 2:1-23

Jesus's mother came from Nazareth, but Jesus was born in Bethlehem: Matthew 2

Jesus's birth foretold four hundred years earlier: Micah 5:2

Augustus's census: Luke 2:4

Jesus's trip to Egypt: Matthew 2:13-15

God is over every land and all people, creator of everything, seen and unseen: Genesis 1, John 1:1-5

Abraham called from Ur to become the father of the people through whom God chose to reveal Himself: Genesis 13

Prophesy about what Jesus would do: Isaiah 53

God's command not to murder: Exodus 20:13

Chapter 14

Moses delivering God's order and God forcing Pharaoh to free the Israelite slaves: Exodus 5-14

Paul's conversion and commission to spread the gospel to the Gentiles: Acts 9, 22:1-21

People who saw Jesus between his resurrection and ascension: 1 Corinthians 15:1-11

Chapter 16

No greater love than to lay down one's life for another: John 15:12-13

Jesus as the sacrifice on the cross, his body given, his blood as the blood of the new covenant Matthew 26: 26-28, Ephesians 1:7, Colossians 1:13-14

Sacrifice of a perfect animal: Leviticus 1:3-4, 10

Blood that makes atonement for sins: Lev. 17:11, John 6:53-57

A summary of Timon's message to Lusario:

"God's *agape* love is so great that He came to earth Himself as a man, as Jesus. He chose to die as the perfect sacrifice, not just to cover sin but to tear down the barriers between us and God. All we must do is believe." (John 3:16)

"The essence of us, our soul, lives on past our body's death. After we die, we either spend eternity with God or go to a place of outer darkness." (Matthew 8:10-13)

"We make the choice ourselves by accepting the forgiveness of God that Jesus made possible or by rejecting it." (John 3:18)

Works by ancient authors

The paraphrases of what was written by ancient authors are based on my interpretation of the original sources as translated in the Delphi Ancient Classics e-book series.

The direct quotations of the historian Tacitus and the philosopher Seneca are from the following:

Seneca, Lucius Annaeus. Delphi Complete Works of Seneca the Younger (Illustrated) (Delphi Ancient Classics Book 27) . Delphi Classics. Kindle Edition.

Tacitus, Publius Cornelius. Delphi Complete Works of Tacitus (Illustrated) (Delphi Ancient Classics Book 24) (p. 1487). Delphi Classics. Kindle Edition.

The direct quotations of the historians Josephus and Philo in the Historical Note are from the following:

Josephus, Titus Flavius. Delphi Complete Works of Josephus (Illustrated) (Delphi Ancient Classics Book 41). Delphi Classics. Kindle Edition.

Philo Judaeus of Alexandria. Delphi Complete Works of Philo of Alexandria (Illustrated) (Delphi Ancient Classics Book 77). Delphi Classics. Kindle Edition.

The text of the letter of Aristeas was provided by Eusebius.

Eusebius of Caesarea. Delphi Collected Works of Eusebius (Illustrated and Translated) (Delphi Ancient Classics Book 94). Delphi Classics. Kindle Edition.

Most of all, I thank God for the opportunity to tell this story. Since it's the backstory for the men who will return in my next long novel set three years later in Egypt, it's a story of planted seeds but not yet harvested. I hope you'll join me in *River of Life* where that planting will finally bear fruit.

No one can write the best book possible without the help of many others. Here are a few who helped me more than I can fully express.

I'm especially thankful for Lisa Garcia. She's a dear friend and my top alpha beta who's helped me with every book in the series. I can feel her prayers while I'm writing the spiritual scenes, and her suggestions always help those conversations have the ring of truth. When it comes to spotting typos, she's as good as a copy editor. Her friendship and prayers bless me in writing and in life.

I want to thank Sherril Odom, who's done a great job as alpha beta for *Honor Bound, Hope's Reward, More Than Honor, What Matters Most, Truth and Honor,* and *Crushed Hopes*. Her eye for what's not quite working helps me find the right fix. I especially value her insights and her prayers when I'm writing the spiritual conversations. Having Sherril on my team is a true blessing.

Christine Dillon, the inspiring author of the Grace series and the new Light of Nations series of Biblical fiction, brings an author's eye and the spiritual insight of a missionary to her work as a beta reader. I feel blessed to have her help, especially with the deeper spiritual sections and as my writing buddy.

Terry Shoebotham is my kindred spirit, local writing buddy, and prayer partner for so much of life. Every author should have a Terry to share about books and life in general, especially over a plate of Chinese or Indian food.

I want to thank Andrew Budek-Schmeisser for being my prayer partner and good friend as I've written so many of these books. It wouldn't be possible to write the spiritual conversations without prayer, and the prayers I need for anything are only an e-mail to Andrew away.

Thanks also to Mesu Andrews for praying with me for inspiration and greater efficiency as I try to create these stories with much less writing time than I used to have. As a leading writer of Biblical fiction, she truly understands how we rely on God's inspiration to get things right. It's wonderful to have someone who also shares my delight in archeological discoveries from Old Testament and Roman times.

I asked Roseanna White, who has designed the rest of the series covers, to make a simpler cover style for this novella/short novel. She made a beautiful cover that captures the feeling of Roman Egypt that's different yet consistent with the covers of the longer novels. As always, she's been a delight to work with, and I treasure her prayers when I'm writing the hard parts.

I also thank my family (son Paul, daughter Lydia, her husband Paul, and granddaughter Payton) for the balance and joy they bring to my life.

But my greatest thanks to go my amazing husband, Jim, who mostly manages not to roll his eyes after hearing the next small variation on the same scene for the nth time. He makes every day a little bit better just by being here. His kindness, patience, and humor provide a model for the best of my heroes. I'm truly blessed to be his wife.

Carol Ashby has been a professional writer for most of her life, but her articles and books were about lasers and compound semiconductors (the electronics that make cell phones, laser pointers, and LED displays work). She still writes about light, but her Light in the Empire series tells stories of difficult friendships and life-changing decisions in dangerous times, where forgiveness and love open hearts to discover their own faith in Christ. Her fascination with the Roman Empire was born during her first middle-school Latin class. A research career in New Mexico inspires her to get every historical detail right so she can spin stories that make her readers feel like they're living under the Caesars themselves.

Read her articles about many facets of life in the Roman Empire at carolashby.com, or join her at her blog, The Beauty of Truth, at carol-ashby.com.

LIGHT *in the* EMPIRE SERIES

Dangerous times, difficult friendships,
lives transformed by forgiveness and love.

The Light in the Empire Series follows the interconnected lives of several Roman families during the reigns of Trajan and Hadrian. Join them as they travel the Empire, from Germania and Britannia to Thracia, Dacia, North Africa, Egypt, Judaea and, of course, to Rome itself.

Although each can be read stand-alone, here are some groupings based on the appearance of some characters in more than one story.

Drusus family: *The Legacy, True Freedom, Second Chances, Forgiven*

Lentulus family: *Blind Ambition, Faithful*

Crassus family: *Blind Ambition, Faithful, Honor Bound*

Sabinus family: *The Legacy, Honor Bound, More Than Honor, What Matters Most*

Glabrio family: *What Matters Most, Truth and Honor*

Titianus family: *True Freedom, More Than Honor, What Matters Most, Truth and Honor*

Brutus family: *Faithful, True Freedom, Honor Bound*

The Dacians: *Hope Unchained, Hope's Reward, True Freedom*

For more relationships based on time, location, and the people involved, visit https://carolashby.com/novel-re-lationships/

Forgiven

Are some wounds too deep to forgive?

With a ruthless father who murdered for the family inheritance, Marcus Drusus plans to do the same. In AD 122, Marcus follows his brother Lucius to Judaea and plots to frame a zealot for his older brother's death. But the plan goes awry, and Lucius is rescued by a Messianic Jewish woman. Her oldest brother is a zealot and a Roman soldier killed her twin, but Rachel still persuades her father Joseph to put his love for Jesus above his anger with Rome and hide Lucius until he heals.

Rachel cares for the enemy, and more than broken bones heal as duty turns to love. Lucius embraces Joseph's faith in Jesus, but sharing a faith doesn't heal all wounds. Even before revealed secrets slice open old scars, Joseph wants no Roman son-in-law. With Rachel's zealot brother suspecting he's a Roman officer and his own brother planning to kill him when he returns, can Lucius survive long enough to change Joseph's mind?

If you're wondering what made the Drusus brothers become what they are, you can find out in *The Legacy*, set eight years earlier, and *True Freedom*, set four years earlier.

Blind Ambition

Sometimes you have to almost die to discover how you want to live.

It's AD 114 in the Roman province of Germania Superior, and being a Christian carries a death sentence. Tribune Decimus Lentulus is on the fast track for a stellar political career back in Rome. When he's robbed, blinded, and left for dead, a young German woman who follows the Way finds him. Valeria knows it's his duty to have her and her family killed, but she chooses to obey Jesus's command to love her enemy and takes him home to care for him.

It's not his miraculous recovery that shakes Decimus to his core. It's the way they love him like family and their unconcealed love for Jesus. In spite of himself, he falls in love with the Christian woman Rome wants him to kill. Can Valeria hide her faith to follow him into the circles of Roman power? Or should he abandon his ambition to help rule the Empire and choose to follow a different way?

Discover what happened to the people of *Blind Ambition* eight years later in *Faithful*.

The Legacy

When Rome has taken everything, what's left for a man to give?

Betrayed by a ruthless son who'll do anything for power and wealth, Publius Drusus faces death with an unanswered prayer—that his treasured daughter, Claudia, and honorable son, Titus, will someday share his faith. But who will lead them to the truth once he's gone?

Claudia's oldest brother Lucius arranged their father's execution to inherit everything, and now he's forcing her to marry a cruel Roman power broker. If only she could get to Titus—a thousand miles away in Thracia. Then the man who secretly told her father about Jesus arranges for his son Philip to sneak her out of Rome and take her to the brother she can trust.

A childhood accident scarred Philip's face. A woman's rejection scarred his heart. Claudia's gratitude grows into love, but what can Philip do when the first woman who returns his love hates the God he loves even more?

Titus and Claudia hunger for revenge on their brother and the Christians they blame for their father's deadly conversion. When Titus buys Miriam, a secret Christian, to serve his sister, he starts them all down a path of conflicting loyalties and dangerous decisions. His father's final letter commands the forgiveness Titus refuses to give. What will it take to free him from the hatred poisoning his own heart?

Join the people you met in *Second Chances* eight years earlier in this tale of betrayal, hatred, love, and forgiveness, where even bad things can work together for good.

Faithful

Is the price of true friendship ever too high?

In AD 122, Adela, the fiery daughter of a Germanic chieftain, is kidnapped and taken across the Roman frontier to be sold as a slave. When horse-trader Otto wins her while gambling with her kidnappers, he entrusts her to his friend and trading partner, Galen. Then Otto is kidnapped by the same men, and Galen must track them half way across the Empire before his best friend loses a fight to the death in a Roman arena.

Adela joins Galen in the chase, hungry for vengeance. As the perilous journey deepens their friendship, will the kind, faithful man open her eyes to a life she never dreamed she'd want?

A trip to the heart of the Empire poses mortal danger to a man who follows Jesus, especially when he must seek the help of an enemy of the faith for Otto to survive. Tiberius hunted Christians when he governed Germania Superior and banished his own son when he became one.

When Tiberius learns sparing Galen offers a chance at reconciliation, he joins the trio on their journey home. Can his animosity toward the followers of Jesus survive a trip with the Christian man whose courage and faithfulness demand his respect?

Follow the continuing saga of the people you met in *Blind Ambition* from the frontier of Germany to the heart of the Empire in *Faithful*.

Second Chances

Must the shadows of the past destroy the hope of the future?

In AD 122, Cornelia Scipia, proud daughter of one of Rome's noblest families, learns her adulterous husband plans to betroth their daughter to the vicious son of his best friend. Over her dead body! Cornelia divorces him, reclaims her enormous dowry, and kidnaps her own daughter. She plans to start over with Drusilla a thousand miles away. No more husbands for her. But she didn't count on meeting Hector, the widowed Greek captain of the ship carrying her to her new life.

Devastated by the loss of his wife and daughter, Hector's heart begins to heal as he befriends Drusilla. Cornelia's sacrificial love for Drusilla and her courage and humor in the face of the unknown earn his admiration…as a friend. Is he ready for more?

Marriage to the kind, honest sea captain would give Drusilla the father she deserves…and Cornelia the faithful husband she's always longed for. But while her ex-husband hunts them to drag Drusilla back to Rome, secrets in Hector's past and the chasm between their social classes and different faiths erect complicated barriers to any future together. Will God give two lonely hearts a second chance at happiness?

Join the people you met in *The Legacy* eight years later in this tale of healing and new beginnings. Surprising things happen when God opens the door.

True Freedom
The chains we cannot see can be the hardest ones to break.

When Aulus runs up a gambling debt to his father's political enemy, he's desperate to pay it off before his father returns to Rome. His best friend Marcus suggests they fake the kidnapping of Aulus's sister Julia and use the ransom money. But when the man they hired kidnaps her for real, Aulus is catapulted into a desperate search to find her.

Torn from his childhood home by Rome's conquering armies and sold as a farm slave to labor until he dies, Dacius's faith gives him strength to bear what he must and serve without complaining. After a deadly accident makes him one of Julia's litter bearers, he overhears Marcus advising her brother to kidnap her. When Dacius almost dies thwarting the kidnapping, a Christian couple pretend Julia and Dacius are their children to keep her brother from finding them before her father returns.

But pretending to be free again makes returning to slavery more than Dacius can bear, while acting like a common woman opens Julia's eyes to dreams and destinies she never knew existed. With her brother closing in and her father almost home, can she find a way around Roman law and custom to free them both for the future they long for?

Find out what happens to Ariana's brother Diegis from *Hope Unchained* twelve years later in this tale of hope and a future never imagined until God opens the door.

Hope Unchained
Can the deepest loss bring the greatest gain?

Rome's conquering army took Ariana's family and freedom, but nothing can take her faith in Jesus. When she rescues a tribune's wife from certain death, her reward is freedom and a chance to free her brother and sister. But first she must catch up with the slave caravan before they vanish forever, and tracking them from Dacia to the coast seems impossible for one woman alone.

Discharged from the legion with a hand crippled by a Dacian knife, Donatus faces a future without hope. When the tribune asks him to escort Ariana on her quest, it's the only work he can find. It means four weeks with a Dacian woman and a gladiator bodyguard, but it takes money to eat. A man without options must take what he can get.

But a lot can happen in four weeks. Even battle-hardened men can be touched by love and forgiveness, and it's easier to face an enemy with a sword than to face the truth. When his moment of truth comes, what will Donatus choose, and what will that mean for both of them?

If you read *True Freedom* and wondered what happened to Leander's beloved sister Ariana, you can find out in *Hope Unchained*. If you wonder what happened to Ursus from *Hope Unchained*, he's the hero in *Hope's Reward*.

Honor Bound

Honor had forced him to protect her. Time would tell if he'd regret it.

Marcus Brutus owns estates, ships, and gladiator schools that increase his fortune daily, but his greatest treasures are his honor and his wife. When she reveals her faith in Jesus before dying after the birth of their son, he's consumed by hatred for the unnamed Christian woman who led his beloved to abandon the Roman gods, making him lose her in this life and the next.

For fifteen years, Licinia's father hid her Christian faith. But now her father is dead, and a ruthless political enemy is hunting for anything to destroy her brother. When she becomes the target, her brother sends her to their estate in Germania. But is that far enough to protect her from an evil man who will stop at nothing?

When a carriage accident leaves Brutus injured and his best friend near death after rescuing Brutus's son, Licinia welcomes and cares for them. But her strange habits and his friend's unexpected recovery make Brutus suspect she's the Christian who corrupted his wife. When her brother's enemies come for her, does honor require him to protect her or turn her over as an enemy of Rome? And when Licinia's heart is drawn toward the pagan man who makes money off death, can she reconcile her growing affection with her love for Christ?

If you read *True Freedom* and wondered what happened to Africanus and Brutus, you can find out in *Honor Bound*.

Hope's Reward

Must the secrets we hide destroy our hope for a future?

For a gladiator slave, each time you step on the sand, it's kill or die. When Ursus decides to follow Jesus, he must choose to die the next time he's ordered to fight…or run away. He runs, taking again his childhood name, Matti. But he isn't just trying to escape. He's running to Thessalonica, where he hopes to find other Christians like the woman who led him to faith.

When Felicia's new husband, Falco, almost kills her in a fit of rage, her uncle won't help her end the marriage with his business partner. He will send her to her sister in Thessalonica, but only if she tells no one she plans to divorce Falco and demand her dowry back before she gets there. When Matti interrupts a robbery too late to save Felicia's money for traveling by sea, he offers to bodyguard and escort her overland to their mutual destination.

After Matti risks everything to save her from Falco's assassins, Felicia fears taking the danger to her sister's family. When his Christian friends take them in, she discovers the deepest desires of her heart. But will the secrets of Matti's past make a future together impossible?

If you wonder what happened to Ursus in *Hope Unchained*, he's the hero in *Hope's Reward*.

More Than Honor

Duty and honor had anchored his life,
but only truth could set him free.

Devotion to duty and dogged determination make Tribune Titianus the most feared investigator of the Urban Cohort. Honor drives him to hunt down anyone who breaks Roman law, but it becomes personal when Lenaeus, his old tutor, is murdered in his own classroom. Why kill a respected teacher of the noble sons of Rome, a man who has nothing worth stealing and no known enemies? Had he learned something too dangerous to let him live?

Pompeia was only a girl when Titianus studied with Father before her family became Christians. She and her brother Kaeso can't move their school from the house where their father was killed. But what if the one who killed Father comes to kill again? Kaeso's friend Septimus insists they spend nights at his father's well-guarded home. But danger lurks there as well. As Titianus hunts for the murderer, will he discover their secret faith and arrest them as enemies of the Empire?

When Titianus gets too close to finding the killer, the hunter becomes the hunted. While he recovers at his cousin Septimus's house,

Pompeia becomes the first woman to touch his heart. But a tribune's loyalty is sworn to Rome, no matter how he feels. When her faith is revealed, will truth and love mean more to him than honor? Does honor require more than devotion to Rome?

If you're curious about what happened with Manius's family, Kaeso's family, and Titianus a year before *What Matters Most*, you can find that story in *More Than Honor*.

What Matters Most

When faced with impossible choices,
how do you decide what matters most?

For ten years, the incorruptible Tribune Titianus enforced Rome's laws. He's four days from leaving the Urban Cohort to teach at his brother-in-law Kaeso's school when Emperor Hadrian and the Praetorian Prefect draft him to secretly investigate and thwart an assassination plot…one that might involve his own commander. He can't refuse, but if Hadrian's enemies discover his Christian faith, will it mean death for everyone he loves?

Titianus's cousin Sabina returns as a widow to her father's house after six years of misery in a marriage that sealed a political alliance. She's dreading the next marriage Grandfather will arrange with someone seeking his support. When her brother's best friend Kaeso offers the encouragement and friendship she's longed for, can she escape the chains of society's expectations to gain what her heart desires?

The new tribune Glabrio wants two things as Titianus trains him: to discover for their commander who Titianus is investigating and to gain the support of Titianus's powerful relatives. Marrying

Sabina would secure the backing of her grandfather, but because of the teacher, she's making choices no noblewoman should. As he gets closer to both his goals, will he realize in time what matters most? If you're curious about what happens to Glabrio in his next assignment, you can find that story in *Truth and Honor.*

Truth and Honor

Is truth worth the price if it costs you everything?

For Tribune Glabrio, descended from three consuls of Rome and determined to be the fourth, commanding the troops policing Carthago appears ideal for hastening his political rise. Arriving from Rome with the secretly Christian Sartorus as his aide, Glabrio discovers the man he was to replace has vanished without a trace. Was the missing tribune too close to finding the counterfeiters Glabrio is now hunting? But no matter the cost, duty and honor require him to enforce Roman law.

Orphaned as a child and taken to live with her pagan grandfather, Martina met Jesus through her step-grandmother. Their faith was a well-kept secret, even from most of their family. With both grandparents now dead, her uncle helps Martina hide the faith he doesn't share. But after a single dinner at her uncle's, the new tribune is determined to get to know her. No matter what she does to discourage Glabrio, he won't leave her alone. But if he discovers her faith, will it mean her death?

When Martina rescues Glabrio from the counterfeiter's schemes, he learns the people who risked everything to save him share the faith that got his grandfather executed. Embracing that faith could cost him the future he planned on. As an officer of the empire, it's his duty to reject it…but what if it's true?

If you're curious about what happened between Glabrio, Titianus, Kaeso, and their families almost a year before *Truth and Honor*, you can find that story in *What Matters Most*.

I'd Love to Hear from You!

If you enjoyed this book, it would be a real gift to me if you would post a review at the retailer you purchased it from. A good review is like a jewel set in gold for an author. Other great places to share reviews are Goodreads and BookBub. If you've read others in the series, it would be great if you post a review of those, too.

I'd also love to hear from you at carol-ashby.com or directly at carol-lashbyauthor@gmail.com.

Want to hear about upcoming releases in the Light in the Empire series and free gifts only for newsletter subscribers?

For free gifts and other special offers, advance notices of upcoming releases, and info about my latest writing adventures, I hope you'll sign up for my newsletter at carol-ashby.com.

Who would you like to see in a future story?

Help me pick what to write next!

Since *Crushed Hopes* is the backstory of several of the men who'll be major characters in *River of Life* (releasing in 2024), I already know which story I'll be writing next. But I'm always looking for the next hero or heroine, and fans of the books in the series often tell me who needs to come back as a story lead.

I delight in responding to those requests. People who loved Galen as a teen in *Blind Ambition* asked to see him as a grown man, and he returned in *Faithful*, a story set eight years later when his faith in God and loyalty to a friend made a world of difference to three other people. Fans of Brutus and Africanus in *True Freedom* learned their fate in *Honor Bound*, and anyone who wondered where Ursus the gladiator in *Hope Unchained* went could find out in *Hope's Reward*.

Sometimes it's what happened earlier that people long to know. So many people asked what happened to Leander's long-lost sister in *True Freedom* that I couldn't resist giving Ariana her own story in *Hope Unchained*.

If you've already read *Truth and Honor* set in Carthago, you might have wondered about Volero's son, who was expected to re-turn shortly from Alexandria in Egypt. You'll be able to find out soon in *River of Life*, the next full-length adventure in the Light in the Empire series that's set in Roman Egypt. I hope this backstory of how Caelus and Lusario got together and became friends has whetted your appetite for finding out what happens three years in the future, a year after Grandfather has died.

There are many more characters in the books of the series that I would like to spend more time with, and I hope there are some for you, too. Who would you most like to see in a future story? What was it about them that made you want more of them? I'd love to hear what you think. It will guide what I write after *River of Life*.

Some possibilities:

Aulus of *True Freedom?*

Septimus or Manius of *Honor Bound, More Than Honor,* and *What Matters Most?*

Someone else I haven't mentioned? (I can't wait to see who shows up here!)

Please tell me who you'd love to see again as a comment at carol-ashby.com or directly at carolashbyauthor@gmail.com!

Sign up for the newsletter at my website, and you'll be among the first to find out what's coming next. Looking forward to hearing from you!

Please tell me who you'd love to see again as a comment at carol-ashby.com or directly at carolashbyauthor@gmail.com!